IN HER WAKE

IN HER WAKE

A *Ten Tiny Breaths* Novella

K.A. TUCKER

ATRIA PAPERBACK

NEW YORK   LONDON   TORONTO   SYDNEY   NEW DELHI

ATRIA PAPERBACK
A Division of Simon & Schuster, Inc.
1230 Avenue of the Americas
New York, NY 10020

First Atria Paperback edition February 2015

ATRIA PAPERBACK and colophon are trademarks of Simon & Schuster, Inc.

For information about special discounts for bulk purchases, please contact Simon & Schuster Special Sales at 1-866-506-1949 or business@simonandschuster.com.

The Simon & Schuster Speakers Bureau can bring authors to your live event. For more information or to book an event, contact the Simon & Schuster Speakers Bureau at 1-866-248-3049 or visit our website at www.simonspeakers.com.

Cover design by Ana Dorfman
Cover photograph © Liam Norris/Plainpicture/Cultura

Manufactured in the United States of America

10 9 8 7 6 5 4 3 2 1

Library of Congress Cataloging-in-Publication Data is available.

ISBN 978-1-4767-8430-4
ISBN 978-1-4767-8429-8 (ebook)

To Lia and Sadie

May this never be your story

I destroyed her life and then got caught in her wake.
And I realize now that it's exactly where I'm meant to be.

Chapter 1

April 26, 2008

"Last one and then we're heading out."

"You're kidding me, right?" Derek's deep voice carries over the steady thrum of house music. He hands off an empty beer bottle to a passing buddy in exchange for two full ones, tossing one to me. "It's what," he glances at his watch, "only *twelve*. And we drove an hour to get here!"

Twisting the cap off, I suck back a big gulp, the fresh, cold liquid like icy relief on a scorching day. Even though it's April in Michigan and barely tipping the freezing mark outside, it's sweltering hot in here. "I warned you that I wanted an early night. I'm hitting the books first thing tomorrow morning or I'm screwed." Four finals in three days. I'm screwed either way. That's probably why the Millers are going down so damn fast tonight. I'm definitely more relaxed than I was when we first arrived.

"You'll be home by tomorrow morning. Until then . . ." He gives his cousin's living room—jam-packed with a blend of college kids and locals—a once-over, stalling on two blonds who look like they could still be in high school.

"If we don't head out soon, I'll be a write-off and you know it." It's no surprise that Derek's busting my balls to stay. He's never been one to miss a party. Normally we have to pry him off the keg. But I only agreed to watching the hockey game—the Red Wings are in the play-offs, after all—and somehow it turned into *this*. If it weren't my last Friday night in Michigan, I would have said no in the first place. "Don't you have finals to worry about, too?"

Derek shrugs, taking another long drag of his beer and then settling his eyes on the brunette tucked into the tight space beside me on the couch. Michelle, I think she said her name was. She's pretty and sweet, and she's casually nudged her thigh against mine enough times for me to know she's into me. But, even though it's been six weeks since Madison came to visit me and I'm dying to get laid, I'm not about to cheat on my girlfriend. Especially not for a one-nighter.

I ignore Derek's dumb smirk. "Where's Sasha?"

He dips his head to the left. I follow his lead to where our friend stands toe-to-toe with a brawny guy wearing a blue Wolverines T-shirt, their lips moving fast and tight. If I had to guess, their little "chat" has something to do with our bowl game against the other Michigan college football team three months ago—which we won—and things are about to heat up. It doesn't help that Sasha wore his "Spartans rule, Wolverines drool" shirt tonight, knowing we were heading into U of M territory.

"Great," I mutter, dragging my six-foot-three-inch frame off the couch. The room sways and I stumble slightly, my foot bumping the tidy line of empties on the floor.

I've had way more than I planned on having in the last four hours.

Shit.

I'm the DD tonight.

I guess that means we're stuck here for a while. And I've probably just fucked myself over for finals.

Wandering over to Sasha, I drop my hand on his shoulder, getting a good grip in case I have to pull him back. Sasha's no runt, only an inch short of matching my height and, thanks to an intense off-season practice schedule, just as built. He can handle his own. I should know; we've been roughhousing together since we were in diapers.

"We all good here?" I eye the guy in front of him, an olive-skinned Latino with a unibrow and an intimidating scowl. I don't recognize his face from the field. Then again, we all wear helmets and I don't waste my time on anything but which number I need to take out.

Sasha thrusts a hand through his shaggy brown hair—almost identical to mine in color—but doesn't answer me, eyes locked on the other guy. I've seen him like this before. It almost always ends up in a fight.

"Sash? Finals start next week," I remind him. They'll be hard enough without swollen eyes and split lips. Plus, I can't be getting into a fight with my healing shoulder.

"Yeah." The word drags on Sasha's tongue and then he smirks. "We're good. Just sharing some helpful tips. You know, the basics. Like how to throw a fucking ball to your receiver."

I step in between them to serve as a barrier just as the other guy leans in.

Thankfully, Derek's cousin, Rich—a big guy himself—strolls out from the kitchen then. "Take it outside. I don't want my place trashed."

Sasha's hands lift, palms out, in an act of surrender. "Nothing to take outside. We're good." Slapping Rich's hand in a friendly way, he leads me away. But not before tossing a wink over his shoulder at Unibrow.

I shake my head but I'm chuckling. "You're a dick. You know that?" When you've lived next to a guy for eighteen years, shared hockey pucks and bloody noses and secrets about rounding bases with girls in school, you can say that without repercussions.

Sasha's the brother I never had.

His smug smile hasn't faded. "I know. And we probably need

to get the fuck out of here now because I just gave that asshole the gears. He's gonna pummel me soon, no doubt. *I'd* hit me if I were him."

"Sorry, man. We're stuck here for a bit. I lost track of the beers." This sucks. I really just want to get home. Maybe Rich knows of a sober girl here that Sash can hit up. Maybe—

"I'll drive," Sasha offers.

"Seriously? You good?" That *would* make things easier.

"Yeah. I've been chugging water for the past hour. I've got finals to worry about, too."

My body sags with relief.

"Come on." He jerks his head toward the door and holds his hand out. "Let's go."

"All right." I slide the keys of my Suburban out of my jeans pocket. It's actually my dad's SUV. We swapped cars over spring break so I can haul back the essentials when I head home for the summer.

I toss them to Sasha.

He has to dive to catch them, taking a few quick steps to regain his balance as he stands upright. "Forgotten how to throw already?" he mutters with a grin.

■ ■ ■

"Stay for summer classes!" Sasha drops the SUV into fourth gear as the quiet, dark road opens up into a long stretch toward Lansing and our apartment near the Michigan State campus. He's still pissed that I'm going back to Rochester until July. When I told him, he didn't talk to me for two days.

We've never had a choice but to stay in Lansing, what with the football summer training schedule. But then I tore my rotator cuff in the last bowl game and had to have surgery to repair it over spring break, so I'm out for the time being. Maybe for good.

Secretly, I'm happy to be going home for a while. I'm even happier that I won't be pushing sleds uphill and running hundred-yard sprints every day at six a.m. As good as I am at the game—and I'm good, otherwise I would never have made a team like the Spartans in the first place—I never held any ambitions to go beyond college ball.

Still, Sasha and I have never been apart for more than a week.

"Nah . . . Madison would *kill* me if I changed my mind now." I let my spinning head fall back against my headrest and close my eyes. I could pass out right here. Maybe I'll get a half-decent night's sleep tonight after all.

"She can come visit," Sasha grumbles.

Derek's loud bark of laughter erupts from the backseat. "You actually wanna listen to Cole givin' it to your little sister in the room next to you?"

"Shut the fuck up, Maynard." I crack an eye to see Sasha's knuckles white against the steering wheel. It took Sasha the better part of a year to come to terms with me dating Madison. Four years later, he still gets uptight with any conversation that even hints at his sister getting laid.

"It's just for a few months, bro. I'll be back at the apartment before you know it," I say, trying to ease Sasha's ire.

"Well, I for one am happier than a pig in shit that you'll be gone," Derek announces. When I let the guys know, Derek immediately jumped on the chance to take my room. He lives with his parents in a small house just outside Lansing and, though his folks are nice, I don't blame him for wanting some space.

I've known Derek for almost as long as I've known Sasha. Derek's family lived with his grandparents three doors down from my parents for a few years while Derek's dad struggled to keep a job in the failing IT industry. Apparently my mom went to welcome them—an apple pie in hand and me clinging to her leg—and Derek greeted us in a pink polka-dot dress. By choice. I don't remember it, but Sasha and I sure as hell have teased him enough about it over the years. I'm kind of surprised he kept in touch with us after they moved to Lansing.

I chuckle. "Have at 'er. Just leave it clean."

"Are you sure you want to agree to that, Cole?" Sasha chuckles. "You've seen what he picks up."

"Hey now . . ." Derek's warning tone only spurns Sasha on.

"What was the last one's name? Tia? Ria?"

"Sia."

"Sia," Sasha echoes. "That chick was—"

■ ■ ■

Hi, my name is Tara. I'm a paramedic. Can you hear me? You were in an accident. We're going to help you.

Hi, my name is Tara. I'm a paramedic. Can you hear me? You were in an accident. We're going to help you.

"Hi, my name is Tara. I'm a—"

"What?" The single word scratches my throat. I open my eyes to the dark sky hanging over me, flashes of red and blue light pulsing rhythmically within my peripherals. Wailing sirens assault my ears, both distant and approaching.

So many sirens.

A woman leans over me. She locks eyes with me and speaks in a calm voice. "Hi, I'm Tara. I'm a paramedic. You were in an accident. Everything is going to be okay. Can you tell me your name?"

I pause, struggling to process her words. "Cole." It hurts to swallow.

Someone else is crouched beside me. I try to turn my head to see who it is, to figure out what's going on.

But I can't turn my head.

"Just hold still, Cole," Tara says as something tightens across my chin. It's then that I notice the stiff brace wrapped around my neck.

"What happened?"

"You were in a car accident, but don't worry. We're going to get you to a hospital real soon." An ambulance's ear-piercing wail abruptly cuts off behind me as brakes squeak.

"How bad is it?" Besides the pain in my neck, I can't feel much of anything else.

"We just need to finish securing your neck as a precaution," she explains, not answering my question, as the other person tightens a strap over my forehead.

Car.

I was in the car.

Who was I in the . . .

Sasha.

Derek.

"Where are they?" My eyes strain, first to the left and then to the right, but I can't see anything. "Where are my friends?"

"Everyone is being taken care of, Cole. Do you know what month it is?"

I have finals next week. Yes. I need to get back for finals. "April."

"Good. Who is the president of our country, Cole?"

"Bush."

"And how old are you, Cole?"

She keeps using my name. Why does she keep doing that? "Twenty. Twenty-one in December."

The other paramedic finishes working on the straps. Hands that I didn't realize were holding my head in place disappear as Tara offers me a sad smile. "Do you remember where you were tonight?"

"A party. At Rich's house." I pause. "Where's Derek? Sasha?"

"There are several paramedics on-site. Everyone is being

taken care of." She calls out to someone unseen, "Can we get him out of here?"

A gruff "yes" answers and suddenly I'm moving. Low voices and competing emergency lights surround me from all angles. I search with my eyes—the only part of my head that I can move besides my mouth—to catch a glimpse of something. Anything. But the straps pin me down tight.

"They'll bring my friends to the same hospital, right?"

"They'll get the best care possible," Tara says, climbing into the back. Again, not really answering my question.

Just as the ambulance doors are closing, a voice crackles over a police radio nearby.

All I catch is "D.O.A." before the locks click shut.

Chapter 2

Brown stains on ceiling tiles.

That's the first thing I see.

My mother's face, her hands clasped and pressed against her lips as if in prayer, is the second.

"Cole, honey?" Her gray-blue eyes widen slightly as she sits up straight in her chair, her blond hair hanging loose around her face. I haven't seen her wear it so casually in public for years.

I blink away the haze in my eyes as I search my surroundings. White walls and light blue curtains. Basic white flannel sheets with thin blue stripes. Machines . . . I'm in a hospital room; that much is obvious. I just don't remember getting here.

What I do know is that I'm in a fuckload of pain. Did someone kick in my chest? Each draw of breath makes me want to hold the next. A slight turn of my neck sends shock waves of agony through my entire right side. It probably has something to do with this sling that's holding my arm in place.

"Carter, he's awake!" my mom calls out as a cool hand embraces mine.

Shoes shuffle against the hospital floor and my dad appears from behind the curtain to stand behind her, his old Stanford Law sweatshirt rumpled and sporting a coffee stain down the front.

The purple bags under their eyes tell me they haven't slept in a while.

"What happened?" My throat is too dry to handle words. I start coughing, only to wince from the pain in my shoulder. Even wincing hurts.

"Here, Cole. You need some water." My mom holds a cup to my lips. "Just small sips for now."

My dad wastes no time, reaching forward to hit the red call button on the bed rail. "The doctors will give you something for the pain."

Taking a few short breaths, I try again. "What happened?"

They exchange glances, and then my dad's Adam's apple bobs with a hard swallow. "You were in a car accident."

"Right." Now I remember the paramedic. That's what she kept telling me. *You were in an accident. We're going to help you.* The pieces start falling into place. The party, the drive home . . .

"You're going to be fine, Cole." My mom squeezes my fingers. "Some bruises and a few broken bones. But you're going to be fine. Just a few days in here and then we can take you home." She repeats in a whisper, "You're going to be fine." I don't know if she's reassuring me or herself anymore, especially with the tears welling in her eyes.

I grit my teeth against the pain as I tip my head to the left, to see the empty bed. "Where's Sasha? They should have put us together." I was eleven the last time I was admitted to a hospital. Sasha and I had decided to race our BMX bikes through a neighbor's pothole-riddled field. We ended up in a room together, both in casts. We've never done anything apart, really.

A nurse in colorful scrubs pushes through the door then to round the bed. "How is our patient?" she asks, her focus on the IV stand next to my bed, checking a myriad of bags, detaching and reattaching drips.

"He's in a lot of pain," my mom answers for me as a short, balding man with a stethoscope around his neck marches in. He lifts a chart board off the bottom of the bed. "Hi. I'm Dr. Stoult. And you are Cole Reynolds . . . twenty years old . . . motor collision." He lifts a sheet to scan the reports, familiarizing himself with me. "How are you feeling, Cole?"

"Like shit."

Normally my mom would reproach me. Now, she just keeps holding my hand like she's afraid to let go.

"Stands to reason. The air bags broke three of your ribs and caused heavy bruising on the left side of your torso and your face. Your clavicle is broken—" He meets my gaze to clarify, "That's your collarbone," before returning to my charts. "You also suffered a minor concussion. Likely from your head hitting the passenger-side doorframe."

"Is that why my head hurts so much?" With everything else, I hadn't noticed the dull throb in the back of my skull until now. It kills.

"Likely. You also had a lot of alcohol in your blood, so some of that may be dehydration. We'll make sure you get plenty of fluids." Hanging my chart back at the end of the bed, he pulls out a thin flashlight. My mom is forced to let go of my hand and step back behind the drawn curtain.

"Clavicle fractures can take upward of twelve weeks to heal. I would recommend you wear your sling as long as possible." He puts the stethoscope against my chest.

"Where are the two guys that came in with me?"

"Try to take a deep breath," the doctor orders.

I do and groan out. He gives the nurse a nod as he adjusts my bandages. She quickly adjusts something on my drip. "There's not much we can do for you except make you comfortable. We're going to up your pain medicine and give you a sedative to help you sleep."

"Can you tell me where my friends are?"

"I'll see what I can find out for you, okay?" He whips open

the curtain and is strolling out of the room before I can offer a "Thanks, Doc."

My mom rushes back to her chair, clutching my free hand once again, her other hand pushing strands of my hair off my forehead. "How long before the sedative kicks in?" she asks the nurse.

"Very soon." The nurse offers me a tight-lipped smile before ducking out of the room, just as my body begins to sink into the mattress, the meds working their magic.

"Dad? Can you find out where Sasha is?" I struggle to form the words, my tongue sluggish. "That doctor probably already forgot."

Silence meets my question.

I fight against the magnetic pull of my lids as I take in two grief-stricken masks. Tears stream down my mom's cheeks. My dad dips his head, his own eyes glossy.

Without their uttering a single word, I hear their answer.

A sob escapes me, even as I feel myself drifting off into oblivion.

But not before I realize that life as I've known it is over.

Chapter 3

The crushing pain in my chest now has little to do with my injuries.

And it's suffocating me.

The clock hanging on the wall opposite me read 3:05 when I regained consciousness. I've watched the second hand do lap after lap for almost twenty minutes now.

Without saying a single word.

My best friends have been dead for almost thirty-six hours.

At some point while I slept, my mom traded her white sweater for a green one and added tear-stained cheeks to the dark bags under her eyes. "Cole. Please say something," she pleads. She never was one for long bouts of quiet, preferring to "talk it out." I took after her in that respect, which probably makes my silence all the more disturbing. My dad, on the other hand, seems quite content to sit on the empty hospital bed behind her, his arms folded across his chest, his face drawn. Mute.

"What happened?"

Mom clears her throat repeatedly. "They were thrown from the truck." A pause. "I don't understand why they weren't wearing their seat belts. We taught you better than that! I just don't—" She cuts herself off as my dad's hand reaches out to graze her shoulder. She purses her lips for a moment as if to compose herself, before continuing. "From what we've heard so far, they died instantly. At least that's . . . that's something." She covers her mouth just as a sob tears out.

A stabbing knot forms in the base of my throat.

"Madison?"

My mom's head bobs. "She came by earlier and will be back later tonight. They're at the apartment, packing up Sasha's things and making arrangements."

"How is she?"

"She's being strong. Cyril said they'll hold off on the funeral until Saturday. Dr. Stoult thinks you'll be released by then," my dad explains, adding, "Derek's going to be buried on Wednesday."

Sasha's and Derek's funerals.

This can't be happening.

"The official police report will be filed shortly but from what they gather, alcohol may have been a fac—"

"No!" I cut him off, clenching my teeth against the pain as I shake my head. "*I* was drunk. That's why Sasha drove in the first place." Sasha wouldn't drink and drive. He's a good guy.

Was a good guy.

"So Sasha *was* driving. They weren't a hundred percent certain if it was Derek or Sasha." My dad's mouth twists. "Regardless, the autopsy reports will confirm how much alcohol was in his blood."

I close my eyes, thinking back to last Friday. Sasha was fine to drive . . . wasn't he? He *said* he was fine, that he had been chugging water. But now that I look back on it, there probably was a beer in his hand most of the night. He could have been nursing it.

Then again, I've never known Sasha to nurse a beer.

Fuck. What was I thinking?

After another long, uncomfortable silence, I finally dare ask, "So, what did we hit, a tree?"

My mom's face pales and I have my answer.

I didn't think I could feel anything through this numbness.

"They're saying that you guys collided with an Audi in the oncoming lane." My dad's eyes are fixed on the floor by my bed, the look in them telling me he's miles away in thought. "There were no skid marks on the road."

Jesus. We plowed into a car with that beast of a truck? "What happened to the other driver?"

Fresh tears spill out from my mom's eyes and that unyielding heaviness against my lungs only grows.

"The police aren't saying too much just yet. All I know is that there were five passengers in the car. Two adults and three teen-agers," my dad explains slowly. "They took a sixteen-year-old girl over to Sparrow. She needed a level-one trauma center."

My stomach drops. "Did she make it?"

"Haven't heard."

"And the others?"

Dark blue eyes—the ones I inherited—lift to meet mine for a moment. So many emotions swirl within them—grief, pity, fear. He shakes his head once.

Five people . . . one survivor . . . That means . . .

Six people now dead.

All because I didn't hold up my end of the deal.

I close my eyes against the rush of emotion.

■ ■ ■

Something silky tickles my fingertips. I don't need to look to rec-ognize the feel of Madison's hair.

A night sky stretches out beyond the vertical blinds. It's nine thirty, according to the wall clock. My parents are gone—hopefully to get some sleep. Madison has taken over for my mom in the chair next to my bed. She's asleep, her head propped in the crook of one arm that rests next to my hip, facing me, her long, poker-straight black hair fanned across my hand. Her face splotchy from crying.

I simply lie there and study her pretty features as she sleeps.

Growing up, I never thought I'd fall in love with Madison. She was always just Sasha's baby sister, hovering in the shadows and blushing whenever she caught our attention. But then that stick-figured, shy kid went away to camp the summer before her freshman year and came back with curves and an impish sparkle in her eye.

No one at our high school recognized her at first, but the guys sure as hell noticed her. I was one of them. *But*, metamorphosis or not, she was still Sasha's sister.

The night that Sasha caught me kissing her in my backyard was the only time he ever took a swing at me with the intention to do some damage. I got the cold shoulder from him for a week after that and I was sure our friendship was over.

He came around eventually, though. After an hour-long speech about how he'd punch me if he ever heard me talking about rounding the bases with her and he'd outright kill me if I hurt her.

I wish he were here to make good on that promise.

Parched, I reach for the cup of water sitting on my bedside table. Except for a few quick, assisted walks around my room, I haven't moved from this bed in two days and I'm beginning to get restless. The nurses have reduced the painkiller dosage and, though my body still hurts, the physical ache isn't nearly as crippling.

When I turn back, Madison's awake, her whiskey-colored eyes on me. I suck in a breath, earning a sharp stab in my chest. I never really noticed just how similar her eyes are to Sasha's.

In fact, they're almost identical.

"Were you guys drunk?" Drops spill down her cheeks. "Did Sasha drive home drunk?"

All I can hear is, "Did *you* let Sasha drive home drunk?"

And the simple answer is yes . . . I did.

．．．

The wood boards creak under my feet as I walk down the front hall of our apartment. Sasha and I moved in here almost two years ago, at the beginning of our sophomore year. Rent's a bit high, but the pub downstairs and the rooftop deck off the kitchen were huge selling features.

I stall in front of Sasha's bedroom, my gaze roaming the vacant space. Everything is gone. Even the thumbtacks that held his posters up. "You guys have been busy." My voice echoes through the space, only amplifying the hollowness in my chest.

"My parents wanted to haul it all back now. You know, get it over with." Madison tucks a strand of her long hair behind her ear. She hesitates for two seconds before closing the distance between us with faltering steps. At five foot one and barely tipping the scale at a hundred pounds, she's tiny next to me. "I've packed most of your clothes up for you. Your mom said to leave the rest over the summer, so it's here for you when you come back in the fall."

Come back. Here.

I scan the room again, testing that notion out. Time stalled when my eyes cracked open in the hospital. Though I feel Sasha's absence like a missing limb, I'm still drifting in a fog. None of this truly feels real yet. Maybe it would be sinking in by now, had I gone to Derek's funeral. I wasn't cleared for release, though. We sent flowers. It hardly seems adequate.

Madison runs her fingertips up and down my good arm in a soothing manner. "Do you think you can handle the drive?" That's my girlfriend. She just lost her only brother and besides one all-out hysterical sobbing episode at the hospital, she has been focused on me the rest of the time.

"No, but it's better than cramming into a plane." And being stared at because of my green-and-yellow mottled face. The six-hour drive from Lansing to Rochester is guaranteed to be un-pleasant, but at least I can stretch out in the backseat. Maybe with the long, drawn-out approach, I can mentally prepare myself for what's to come.

Tomorrow, I will have to see my best friend in a coffin. The day after, I'll have to watch him lowered into the ground.

Heavy steps approach from the doorway. "How many more boxes?"

"Just a few," Madison promises, poking her head past me and into the hall just as my dad appears. "I'll bring the suitcases. They're on wheels."

With a nod of thanks to her, he turns to me. "Are you ready? I imagine we'll need to make a few stops along the way."

"Yeah. Just . . . give me a minute." When Madison hesitates to leave, I add softly, "Alone."

She ducks her head and nods. I can't tell if she's hurt. To be honest, I don't really care right now, as I maneuver around the suitcases and a box of textbooks that block my way into my room. Someone—Madison, I assume—cleaned up, stripping my bed and bagging the dirty laundry I didn't get to. The loose change scattered over my dresser has also been collected into a small glass jar, the trash tossed.

My fingers lock over the smooth cover of my Typography text-book as I step around my packed things. I should have taken that final first thing Monday morning. My mom has already met with my professors and the dean at Michigan State. The paperwork is in place to defer my exams until August, before I'm supposed to start my senior year of classes and college ball. *If* I can play.

But that would mean playing on a team without Sasha.

I've *never* played on a team without Sasha. Our entire child-hood was all about tossing balls and slapping pucks to each other. We came as a pair. When we both tried out as walk-ons freshman year, I accepted the idea of not playing if my best friend didn't also make the team.

Never once have I accepted a life without him.

My mattress creaks under my weight as I sit. *This* is where I was meant to end up that night. Sitting here, on this bed, surrounded by these scuffed navy-blue walls, the muffled hum of voices and music filtering from the bar below, with this damn sharp-cornered textbook jabbing into my legs, while I cursed myself for not studying sooner.

Not being pulled out of my car on the side of the road, my friends' heads having collided with pavement.

The textbook slams into the wall opposite me with a loud thud and a crack, its spine snapping. Quick footsteps rush down the hall and Madison appears in the doorway, her gorgeous face full of panic. When she sees me, her shoulders drop. "Oh, I thought you fell or . . ." She surveys the new and sizeable gouge in the drywall and then the textbook lying below, its pages fanned awkwardly. Her hands at her throat draw my attention to her long, thin neck. I've always found Madison's neck especially alluring, unable to keep my mouth off it for very long. Now, I simply stare at it, thinking how fragile the human body is.

Wondering exactly what broke Derek's neck when he was thrown. Was it the car frame? The ground?

Madison closes a hand over the handle of my suitcase and wheels it out of the room without another word.

I last another ten seconds before I'm swallowing the saliva pooling in my mouth. Wandering into the kitchen, I pop open the fridge, in search of water. Someone's emptied it of pizza boxes. All that's left are a few condiments and a case of Miller Genuine Draft.

Sasha's favorite.

I take the three steps to the kitchen sink and lean over, expecting to puke. Hoping like hell that I don't because with all my injuries, I'll likely pass out from the pain.

"You'll be all right," my mom croons softly, appearing out of nowhere. A cool hand touches the back of my neck, the chill soothing.

"How do you know that?" Because right now I'm wishing I hadn't had my seat belt on either that night.

She offers me a pinched smile that doesn't touch her eyes. "Are you ready to go home?"

"No, but I don't really have a choice, do I?"

Her shoulders hunch as though she has a ten-ton weight sitting on them as she pulls the trash out of the can.

"I'm sorry, Mom."

"I know you are," she whispers, pushing down on the newspaper that pokes out.

"Wait." I rush over and pull the stack out before she has a chance to tie the bag.

Three papers had been tossed. All with front pages covering the same story, none feeling real. But there's my dad's Suburban, the front left corner caved in, the windows all shattered. A second, smaller photo on the inset shows a hunk of twisted metal, the four linked rings—the Audi symbol—hanging off what must be the front grill.

How even one person survived in that is a miracle.

I falter over the headline, "Six Dead in College Drunk-Driving Accident." "How can they print this?" I yell, holding up the paper in front of me. "They haven't proven anything yet!"

My mom's hand closes over the stack, gently tugging the papers. "You shouldn't read those right now."

I tighten my grasp and pull, freeing them from her fingers. Using the counter to spread out the pages, I sift through the articles until I come to a half-page picture of a teenage girl. She's wearing a rugby jersey and she's beaming. "Sixteen-year-old Kacey Cleary from Grand Rapids, Michigan," the byline under the picture reads.

"It says she's still in critical care but they expect her to survive," my mom offers as I scan the article quickly, struggling with each new breath. According to this, they were heading home from a rugby game at a rival school near Detroit. They should have been home earlier, but they stopped for celebratory pizza.

The dead include her parents, her boyfriend, and another teenage girl. Probably her best friend. So, pretty much everyone who's important to a sixteen-year-old.

What will this do to her?

I feel the blood drain from my face. "Does she have other family?"

"An eleven-year-old sister, who's being cared for by an aunt and uncle right now."

Eleven years old. Just a kid. "Should we visit her in the hospital?"

"Your father has tried, but she's not . . . accepting anyone right now." The way my mom's voice falters tells me there's more to that, but I don't push. She holds the trash bag open, waiting for me to deposit the papers. With awkward one-armed movements, I roll the papers up against the counter and tuck the bundle under my armpit instead.

If only they hadn't stopped for pizza.

If only I had remained at home to study.

If only I had stayed sober like I was supposed to.

If only I hadn't handed Sasha the keys.

I leave the apartment, drowning in a sea of "if onlys."

■ ■ ■

My dad makes the familiar turn down Logan.

And my hands are trembling. That's never happened before.

I can drive this street with my eyes closed. Forty feet in is Mr. Peterson's rickety old fence that Sasha and I took out while riding our skateboards. Another fifty feet and I'm staring at Ms. Meddock's big bay window, the one I shattered with a slap shot. Four doors down from that is the family home of Naomi Gomes, our babysitter and the first girl that both Sasha and I ever crushed on. The house next to that used to belong to Derek's grandparents, until they sold and moved to Arizona.

And, at the end of this cul-de-sac, two backsplits sit side-by-side. Both of them homes I would stroll into without a second's thought.

Until now.

Now, my gut constricts at the sight of them. The one on the left sits empty and quiet, a tomb of lifelong memories. The other hosts a steady stream of cars and somber-faced people coming to pay their respects for a tragic loss.

And it finally sinks in.

This is really happening.

Chapter 4

June 2008

"Shouldn't you be wearing your sling?" Madison settles two cans of Coke on the coffee table amidst the stack of textbooks and dishes from lunch . . . and breakfast . . . and yesterday's barely touched meals.

"I needed a break." I also need a break from being a one-armed gimp, but I'm not getting that anytime soon. I can't even kill time and dark thoughts with a damn video game. At least my face doesn't look like it was used as a punching bag anymore and my ribs are on the mend. I'm not struggling to breathe, either. Not physically, anyway.

Stepping over a lazy Murphy—the golden Lab mix that Sasha helped me pick out at the pound eight years ago—Madison falls into the space beside me on the couch. I feel her eyes on me, searching, but I keep my attention glued to the TV screen as I cautiously settle my good arm over her shoulder. I don't know if she's finding any comfort in it. I sure as hell am not.

She deserves a strong chest to lean against and soak up her tears, a sounding board for her frustrations. A boyfriend who will ease her pain after losing her only brother. Not a guy who can't meet those all-too-familiar whiskey-colored eyes for more than three seconds before ducking away.

An awkward silence hangs over us. We're moving into a strange stage of detached grief, where everyone has begun to accept reality. It's impossible not to. Sasha's absence in our lives is like a gaping fissure in the middle of a bridge. How the hell do you cross to get to the other side when you've run out of concrete? I guess you can slap on some wood to patch it up, to help you move on. But the bridge will never be quite right—never as strong—again.

With the acceptance of that reality, a slew of worthless "what ifs" and plenty of angry "whys" have followed from my parents, from Sasha's parents, from Madison. Even from friends.

"*Why* were you out partying before exams in the first place?"

"*Why* weren't they wearing their seat belts!"

"*Why* would you do something so stupid!"

I hear the unspoken accusation in it. I was there. I was as much a part of this as Sasha and Derek. And, though I understand where they're coming from, the words hammer me over the head until I retreat to the sanctuary of this rec room.

"Fitz and Henry texted me," Madison says. "They're having a party this weekend. Wanted to know if we'd come. A lot of the gang will be around."

"I'll catch up with them some other time." I barely said two words to them at the funeral and I haven't answered any of the emails or texts since then.

"Do you want help studying?" She leans forward to flip open a textbook. My mom left my books there about two weeks ago. I haven't cracked a single cover, the very idea of school exhausting.

"Nah, I'm good. Don't you have your own finals to make up, anyway?"

Madison shrugs as her hand falls to rest momentarily on the half-buried newspaper. On the sixteen-year-old survivor's face that stares out at me. I don't feel right using her name yet.

Clearing her throat, she asks quietly, "Should we go see her?" Madison and her parents feel as much pity for the girl as I do. After all, it was her brother, their son, behind the wheel.

"I don't know. She's not accepting visitors right now."
Translation: When my parents flew out there to see her and
the nurse informed her of her guests, the girl screamed at the
top of her lungs until they had to pump a sedative into her
veins. Apparently she demanded that the hospital call the police and, when the cops finally arrived, she spewed all kinds of
threats of bodily harm and murder should any of us step foot
inside her room. With her body set in a cast, she can't even
move right now.

She's been put under psychiatric assessment.

Madison sighs and then nods, scooping up her long jet-black
hair to fasten it with an elastic band.

"You look really nice." I mean it, even though the hollow
sound of my voice makes it sound insincere. Most days she
changes out of her work clothes and into yoga pants and a tank
top before coming. Today, though, she kept her dress on.

"Thanks." A glimmer dances in her eyes. The first one I've
seen since spring break.

"How's the internship going?" I don't think I've even asked
her that question yet. Madison just finished her freshman year in
Washington, D.C., at one of the top journalism programs in the
country. She delayed her start date by two weeks because of the
accident but decided that she needed to work, to keep her mind
occupied. I was supposed to be interning at my mom's creative
agency over the summer. Clearly, I'm not doing that.

"It's good. I work with this team of people. They're really
nice. They . . ." She rambles on about her coworkers and her boss,
and about the article she had to fact-check today. Though I'm
not listening to her actual words, I let the soft hum of her voice
drown the voice spewing dark thoughts within my subconscious,
even if just for a while.

"Who's winning?" she suddenly asks, balling her hands

tightly. A sign that she's irritated. I guess she noticed that I had tuned her out.

"Detroit." The Red Wings—my and Sasha's favorite team and one reason why we chose Michigan State—are about to win the Stanley Cup and I couldn't care less. It's just a way to pass the time for me now.

Suddenly Madison is standing in front of me, blocking my view of the screen. Her bottom lip quivering, her eyes watering. "Do you still want me?" The question is soft, almost a whisper.

I blow a mouthful of air out, sufficiently gutted by how vulnerable she looks right now. "Of course I do, Mads. You know I still do. It's . . ." I dip my head. "It's only been five weeks. And it's just . . ." What is *it*, exactly? I mean, the injuries are real. The grief is real. And the guilt gnaws away at my core.

I lift my gaze to find Madison pulling the sleeves of her blue dress down over the balls of her shoulders. The shape slackens as the material slides over her curves, falling to her ankles. Broken bones or not, blood rushes downward fast as she reaches back to unfasten her bra, letting it drop. Her panties follow.

And then she just stands there, waiting, her fingers twitching nervously at her sides.

I release the air in my lungs slowly as I reach down and un-button my jeans. "I don't know how much you'll enjoy this."

"I want to try." She reaches down as I lift my body to help slide my pants over my hips. Lifting one knee and then the other, she carefully straddles my lap and then edges forward, her breaths coming fast and short.

I'd be lying if I said I didn't want this. Or, that a part of me didn't want this. The evidence is right there, between us.

And yet, it feels all wrong.

Reaching down, she guides me into her. I groan with the feel of her warmth, letting my head fall back into the pillow, and my thoughts scatter.

Maybe this is all I need to start feeling alive again.

■ ■ ■

Hi, my name is Tara. I'm a paramedic. Can you hear me? You were in an accident. We're going to help you.

Her voice, her words, they linger in my mind like a broken record long after I've come to, my body drenched in sweat, my breathing ragged.

It was only a dream, I tell myself.

The worst night of my life is over, I remind myself.

I'm just living in its wake.

Chapter 5

July 2008

"0.14. Almost double the legal limit!"

My bedroom is situated at the back of our house but I have no trouble hearing the words coming from the kitchen, laced with anger.

I guess my dad finally got his hands on the toxicology report.

"Do you know how fast they were going? Dammit! I never thought I'd wish that these trucks weren't built with black boxes." I can picture my dad pacing, his hands resting on his head. It's what he does when he's mad enough to swear, which isn't frequent. "My insurance company is going to have a field day with this! I won't be able to afford the premiums by the time they're done with me. As it is, we're lucky that we had the highest coverage we could possibly have."

"Lucky." Great choice of words, Dad.

"And a lawsuit?" my mom asks.

My dad groans. "What a goddamn mess. Out-of-state accident, our son's friend driving. Drunk! If not for the no-fault insurance laws, we'd be selling our house right now. As it is, the family of that boy—Billy—are looking for more than what the state laws are forcing the Clearys' insurance company to pay out. If they can't get it, then yes, we should prepare ourselves for a lawsuit. Against us and maybe even Cyril and Susan, though that probably won't get too far."

"But it'll still cost them in legal fees, won't it?

"No, it won't. The firm will take care of it. The partners have already agreed to take the hit for billing hours if it comes to that."

"And have you talked to the girl's aunt about the medical bills?"

He sighs. "She isn't getting out of the hospital anytime soon. Our insurance and the family's medical insurance aren't going to cover everything. Her aunt seems willing to refrain from a lawsuit if we help cover those."

"Yes, of course. I suppose that will have to come from our fund?"

"I don't see how we have any other choice."

My stomach curls. "The fund" means only one thing to my parents: their retirement dream—a summer home in Cape Cod, right by the ocean. They started saving for that the day they got married. Loose change at first, neither of them able to set aside much more. Though I don't know exactly how much they have socked away now, I have to expect it's a good chunk. My dad's always been good with managing their money.

Now, not only have I ruined their reality; I've ruined their dreams, too.

There's a pause, and then, "What the hell was Cole thinking, handing the keys to him! The hospital report put him at 0.10. He would have been better off driving himself!"

I crack my door in time to hear my mom's rushed hiss. "Lower your voice! And don't you dare say that! Every time I think about it, I—" Her voice cuts out with a ragged sob. "We could have lost him in that accident, too."

My dad's voice lowers, but I can still hear him. "You don't think we've lost him?"

Her sigh lingers in the air. "It's only been two months. He'll come around."

"Does anyone ever come around from something like this,

Bonnie? *Six* people died. That poor girl is still lying in a hospital bed because of his recklessness."

"It wasn't—"

"He was the damn DD!"

"Enough!" Hearing my mom scream at my dad spikes the hairs on my neck. It's so unlike her. Unlike them, to fight like this.

An eerie silence hangs and then, "Has he even gotten out of bed yet today?"

I glance over my shoulder at the angry red numbers on my clock. Two p.m. To be fair, I didn't fall asleep until after six this morning. Why is my dad even home at two in the afternoon? Unless . . . oh, right, it's Saturday. I've lost track of the days, especially now that Madison has stopped coming over every night after work. She says it's because she's busy. I know she's lying.

Secretly, I'm relieved. Those daily doses of guilt every time she sat down next to me on the couch were getting to be too much.

"Do Cyril and Susan know yet?" my mom asks.

"No. I'm going to go over and tell them now." His shoes drag along the floor as he heads for the front door.

I shut my door and fall back into bed, glad that I didn't bother to pull the curtains open.

■ ■ ■

Hi, my name is Tara. I'm a paramedic. Can you hear me? You were in an accident. We're going to help you.

"I don't need help. I'm fine," I hear myself say. I must be, because there are no straps to hold me back from rolling onto my side, ready to get up. Until I see Sasha lying next to me, his lifeless gaze trained on me.

And suddenly I can't move.

I can't shut my eyes.

I can't even blink.

I can't do anything to get away from Sasha and his dead stare.

■ ■ ■

The grainy newspaper print didn't do her justice.

With its black-and-white limitations, it certainly didn't highlight the sparkle in those pale blue irises, or her hair—the same color as the sweet red peppers my mom has growing in the backyard garden.

Kacey Cleary is pretty. *Really* pretty.

Or, at least she *was*. I have no idea what shape she was in coming out of that wreck, other than "critical." After what we did to her, is the face I'm staring at now still the same? Or has it been horribly mangled? I wonder what she's doing at this very moment, and that constant ball of sickness in the pit of my stomach flares with the thought.

"I thought you said Facebook was stupid?"

I jump at the sudden sound of Madison's voice behind me, the low music playing over the stereo system masking her approach.

"I said it sounded lame." I push the screen down, out of sight. It seems like everyone and their mothers are on Facebook nowadays. Everyone except for me. When I want to talk to my friends, I just pick up the phone. I've never seen the value of this social media phenomenon.

Until now.

Because Kacey has a profile on there. A profile that's not locked down and is bursting with posts and pictures of her—with her friends, her teammates, her family.

The parents, the boyfriend, the best friend who I helped kill.

The little black-haired sister whose face is a carbon copy of hers. Who's now an orphan.

There must be over two hundred pictures posted on here. And I've sat on this couch for days, laptop in hand, memorizing every last one. Kacey and her best friend, Jenny, in bikinis, holding hands and jumping off a rocky ledge into the lake below, their mouths open with exhilarated screams. Kacey, wrestling with her father in the grass and smearing what appears to be melted chocolate all over his nose. Kacey and her boyfriend, Billy, holding hands, laughing, stealing kisses.

Kacey, smiling devilishly at the camera. Always smiling.

Did that smile survive?

Along with the pictures are plenty of posts. Cute banter between her and her best friend, who apparently had a thing for Hannah Montana, while Kacey clearly did not. Hilarious one-liners between her dad and her, where her dad quotes old movies and she gives the most ridiculous answers back. Billy and her trying to outdo each other with the cheesiest "What do you call . . .?" jokes I've ever read.

Thanks to Facebook, I've learned that Kacey has a small army of friends who beg her to hang out with them on weekends. Sometimes she says yes, that Jenny and she will come. It's never just her. And sometimes she says that she's hanging out with her family that day. It's so obvious that the Clearys were tight.

Her last post reads, "Better luck next time, Saints! You can't beat this redheaded Irish girl." It's dated April 25th.

The Friday of the accident.

After that, nothing but an endless stream of well-wishes and prayers from friends and family fill her wall.

There isn't a single response from Kacey.

But there are a slew of condemning messages about "the assholes who did this to you."

"Aren't you sick of the dark?" Madison turns on a table lamp. She shivers against the cool basement air. "It's beautiful out.

Eighty-two degrees and blue skies." Her eyes linger over my unshaven face, my rumpled jeans and T-shirt, and that deep furrow between her brows deepens. "When did you go outside last?"

Murphy hears the word "out" and his head pops up, his tail wagging. I push my laptop closed, half with reluctance and half with relief. "Not today."

Not yesterday either.

I should probably take the poor dog for a walk. I can handle it now. The doctor cleared me for light exercise last week. My body—in decent shape before the accident, despite my shoulder injury—could use it now.

"Are your parents still at the office?" Madison asks as she perches herself on the edge of the couch as if trying to avoid the dirt. Or me.

Hell, I may not have shaved or chosen clean clothes, but I have showered. I don't *think* I smell. I'm half-tempted to take a whiff of myself. But after spending the entire day flogging myself with pictures of dead strangers, I decide that I don't really give a damn.

"Yeah. More and more lately. Dad's got a big case, so . . ." So, he's using it as an excuse to not come home. And when he does make an appearance, he's got a tumbler full of scotch in hand. He doesn't get shit-faced, but it's still concerning. My dad's never been one for hard liquor.

He and my mom also never fought. Sure, they'd have small spats over taking the trash out and lowering toilet seats, but there were never any major blowouts, no name-calling, no arguments that threw the household into a nuclear winter.

Lately, though, fighting is all they seem to do.

Growing up, my parents were the ones all my friends wanted to hang around. They liked to laugh and joke with everyone and never took anything too seriously. My mom was the agreeable chauffeur, and my dad loved swearing at the hockey commentators as much as we did. You'd never even guess that he's a high-priced lawyer and my mom runs her own small but successful design firm. On weekends, my mom could be found in the kitchen with flour on her nose and my dad would spend hours trimming our front hedge to perfection.

He was the husband who made his wife's coffee every morning, because she's not a morning person. She was the wife who ironed his shirts, because he hates ironing. Together, they were the couple who always went to bed together.

But all that has changed.

Silence hangs between Madison and me. I wait for the break in it. I know it's coming. She's picking at her fingernails. She only does that when she's about to do something uncomfortable.

"My grief counselor said she could fit you in, if you're interested in talking to someone."

"I *have* talked to someone." I slide out the bottle from my pocket and give it a shake. The small green-and-white Prozac capsules rattle like a maraca. Apparently they take three to four weeks to take effect. They should be kicking in any time now.

"But you're not getting better."

"Not everyone can forget as easily as you can." The second the words are out of my mouth, the second I see her face crumble, I'm hit with a wave of regret.

"Who *are* you?" she cries out, tears streaming down her cheeks. Madison's never been good with confrontation. "I want *my* Cole back. I can't deal with this one anymore! You're not the only one who lost Sasha!" I don't have a chance to apologize before she's running up the stairs.

I should get up, should chase after her, should apologize over and over again.

But I open my computer up and continue staring at sixteen-year-old Kacey Cleary's bottomless blue eyes instead.

■ ■ ■

I hit "replay" for the tenth time on an old video of a fifteen-year-old Kacey. Her grin is wide as her team's rugby coach gets drenched with a bucket of water. I thought only guys did that sort of thing. That's certainly not the case here, not with her as the team captain, anyway.

It seems like Kacey was a bit of a prankster—the water bucket incident just one of many practical jokes I've found evidence of—which means she must have a wicked sense of humor. I can tell that her teammates really like her. At any given time, she has at least four of them flocking around her. Every time her lips move, they're laughing. An easy, pleasant confidence swirls about her that is so rare around girls, at least any that I've known. Madison sure never had it. She's always been shy and rather oblivious to her appeal. While I adore her charm, there's something decidedly sexy about a girl who's comfortable with herself.

But has that all changed for Kacey?

Chapter 6

"For Sale."

I feel like someone slammed the sign into my gut.

"I never imagined they'd sell. Susan loves that house." My mom sidles up behind me and wraps her arm around my waist as I look out on the Daniels property from our step. "Up one day and the agent already has multiple offers."

I search for the right words but there are none, so I settle on trying to clear the lump in my throat.

"It's nice to see you out here, Cole. You could use some sun." Her hand reaches up to touch my cheek. "And a shave."

The sound of my own name irritates me. At first, it just earned a few raised hairs. Then a prickle. Then a wince. Now, though, I hear "Cole" and I feel like I'm being reprimanded for something horrible that I've done. In my head, that paramedic's voice still says it over and over again, as she tends to me while my friends lie dead mere feet away. While Kacey sits trapped in that car.

When I hear my name, a fresh wave of guilt flows through me. I wish she'd stop using it.

"I saw Madison earlier. She was asking about you. She said you had a fight?"

Aside from a few check-in texts, I haven't talked to her since she ran out of the rec room almost three weeks ago. She's heading back to Washington next Thursday.

Two days before I leave for Michigan State.

There's no physical reason why I shouldn't go back to school. My ribs and my collarbone have set, based on the latest doctor's appointment and X-rays. The doctor even mandated weights to build my muscle back up. He's cleared me for football practice.

Too bad I've already quit the team.

Coach had been sending me emails periodically over the summer, checking in. I finally told him two weeks ago. I don't think he was too surprised. Of course, I haven't told anyone else yet. It doesn't really matter, in the grand scheme of things. I'd just rather forget about football and move on.

I *have* been studying, though. If I took the exams today, I could probably get by with Cs.

"Why don't you go over there and talk to her? Apologize," my mom says with a gentle push against my back.

I sigh, knowing it's time that I got this over with.

■ ■ ■

I remember the last time I actually knocked on this door. I was seven and had just had a huge fight with my dad. Naturally, I snuck out my bedroom window with a bag of clothes and my G.I. Joe figurines, intent on running away. Even more naturally, I headed straight for my second home. I figured knocking on the door was the best opener before I pled my case about why Sasha's parents should let me move in with them. How I didn't eat much and Sasha and I could share a room.

It's the exact same door, only now it's painted black instead of forest green.

It takes a few minutes for it to open and, when it does, it's not Madison standing before me. It's the woman who knows me as well as my own mom does.

"Hello, Cole," Susan Daniels says. I always used to tease Sasha, saying that his mom may "stay at home" but she had a side profession working as a phone sex operator. Pissed him off something fierce. I don't hear the sultriness in her voice now, though.

Her sadness must have stifled it.

Without meaning to, I count the seconds of awkwardness. Three. They feel like thirty.

But then she steps forward and wraps her arms around my neck, forcing me to stoop as she pulls me down into her short body, her grip tightening around my recently healed collarbone.

"I'm so happy to see you," she whispers as she shifts away, her hands stalling on my scruffy cheeks, holding my face in place as she stares up at me, searching. As if those eyes that both of her children inherited are trying to communicate silently with me.

I wonder if she can read the apology within mine.

I don't think I'll ever stop saying I'm sorry.

She smoothes her shirt down over her hips as she backs up, making room for me to walk in. I have to hold my breath as I step over the threshold, as if I can't possibly handle breathing and striding into Sasha's home simultaneously.

She must sense it because she quickly takes my hand and leads me forward, down the hall, past the living room that I hung out in almost every Saturday night of high school, before heading out to a party or a movie or general teenage boy shenanigans. Gone are the stacks of DVD cases and clutter of family photos sitting on the mantel. Gone are the collections of knickknacks and trophies from the bookshelf. The "office" in the corner—a desk normally buried with stacks of papers and stationery, where Cyril does the bulk of his accounting work—is missing. The Daniels home now sits tidy and coordinated and void of its personality, hiding its pain, ready to welcome an oblivious new family.

"Aren't you going to miss it here?" The breath I've been holding escapes with my words, making me sound all husky and emotional.

Her fingers clamp around mine. "I think we could all use a change," is all she says.

Even though I have a damn good idea where she's leading me, my feet still stall as we step into Sasha's room.

Or, what *was* Sasha's room. "It looks different in here." My gaze absorbs the light gray walls, once army green and mottled with dents from the tennis ball Sasha liked to bounce off them, both to relieve stress and to drive his sister—her headboard just on the other side—nuts. The TV and Nintendo, the sports posters, the blue-and-green plaid bedding that he's had in his room since we were thirteen . . . gone.

I don't even recognize the room.

Sasha has been erased. I'm not sure if I have a right to be upset by this, but I am. I bite my tongue against the urge to spew accusations that would be both hurtful and untrue.

Susan opens up the closet and points to a sizeable cardboard box with my name scrawled in black marker on the side. "I was cleaning out his room and I thought these things should go to you. You know . . ." Her lips press together in a tight smile. "A way to remember your friendship. You meant everything to him, Cole."

I know her words are intended to be kind, but she might as well have driven a railroad tie into my throat. Forgetting our friendship will never be a problem for me.

I can't manage a response besides, "Thanks."

"It's heavy. If you need Cyril to carry it over for you, I can—"

"No, I'm good." I'm moving fast, diving down to wrap my fingers around the base of the box and lifting. Because, suddenly, I just want to get the hell out of here.

I step into the hallway, box loaded in my arms, and find Madison in the doorway of her room. Now I remember why I came here in the first place. "Hey, Mads."

"Hey." She dips her head to the side, her eyes meeting her mom's in a silent exchange.

"Well, the open house starts in two hours. I should go and get those cookies in the oven. I read that prospective buyers like that sort of thing." Susan gives my arm one more rub before quietly trailing down the hall.

I make my way into Madison's room, also freshly painted but not as drastically changed. There are still the same floral sheets that she had on that very bed the night she gave me her virginity three years ago.

Madison's throat bobs with a hard swallow as she pushes the door closed behind her. "I didn't mean—"

I cut her off. "I'm sorry about what I said." I'm sorry about so much more. Especially what I'm about to do. My weak arm is starting to ache with the weight of the box. I set it down on the bed and then take a seat next to it. "I know you miss him and you're hurting. Just as much as I am." I rest my elbows on my knees and lean forward, dipping my head down to stare at the wood grain in the floor, so I don't have to face her with my next words. "I don't know how long it's going to take to get my shit together, Mads. I'm only going to drag you down with me while I figure it out."

Soft footfalls approach and she leans in. Her stomach presses against my head and soothing fingertips begin sliding along the back of my neck. "It's okay. I know you didn't mean it. It's just . . . it's so hard to see you like this. I don't know what to do or say. I don't know how to make it better."

"That's the problem, though, isn't it?" I swallow the bile rising as I reach up to take her hands in mine. I lift my head and tip it back to meet her gaze. Those eyes. *Dammit*. I've always thought they were beautiful, and yet now they haunt me. "We should be there for each other through this. But I'm not here for you. I *can't* be here for you. Not right now."

Her bottom lip starts to wobble and a watery film forms over her eyes. She's trying her hardest not to cry. Just like when she was twelve and she tripped on the sidewalk and scraped her knee so badly, she still has a scar from the fall. She admitted years later, after we started dating, that she didn't want me to see her cry because it would remind me that she was just Sasha's dumb little sister. The one who'd had a secret crush on me since she was seven years old.

"What are you saying?"

I pull her tiny, rigid frame into my lap so I can hold her tight. I've known this girl all my life. I've been in love with her for the better part of four years. I turned down countless "opportunities" in college for her. I've thought about our future—marriage, kids, the house. Right down to the cat and dog who would fight at first but eventually learn to cohabitate.

I always said I'd kill anyone who hurt her.

I guess that's what I'm doing now. It definitely feels like another nail in the coffin I climbed into three months ago.

It's been a slow, painful death.

"That I want you to head back to Washington and focus on you and only you. And . . . if you find someone who can be there for you, and who you can lean on, then," I say, though just the idea of her with someone else makes me nauseous, ". . . I'll be happy for you."

"Are you—" She chokes down a sob. "Are you breaking up with me?"

"You've only ever been with me and I don't want you to regret that. To feel trapped with me because of what happened." I say it as softly as I can. "I'm letting you go, Mads."

Her jaw drops as tears begin to roll. "No. No . . . I didn't mean it. I was just upset. We can work through this." She twists her body and finds my cheeks with her hands, closing her mouth over mine, her salty tears coating my lips.

I've already made up my mind. Still, how do you pull away from someone you love this much when you know it's probably the last kiss you'll ever share? And when it deepens, and one of her hands slides under my shirt, I know that I don't have a choice. Open house or not, I'm tempted to have just one more time with Madison in this bed, for old times' sake. But then I'll chicken out.

So, I break away from her mouth to lock eyes with her. It's the least I can do, not turn away from her, as I've been doing all these months. "You've been a hundred feet away from me all summer and I've made no effort. It's only going to get worse and I can't deal with that guilt, on top of everything else. I just . . ." I swallow the lump but it won't budge. My eyes begin to burn as I force out in a whisper, "I'm sorry."

Whatever restraint she held on to before breaks down and a torrent of tears releases. "Please. I can't lose you, too," she gets out between the sobs.

Can't she see it?

She already *has* lost me.

■ ■ ■

My mom leans into my car window. "Are you sure you don't want me to drive out with you? I can fly back."

"I'm good, Mom." I test the feel of the steering wheel under my fingertips. *My* Honda Accord. The car that Sasha would have been driving that night, had I not swapped for my dad's monstrous SUV. It would have caused considerably less damage to the Cleary family's car. Maybe more of them would have survived.

Maybe I wouldn't have.

I've sat in a car only a dozen times this summer, and on only a handful of occasions have I been behind the wheel. Never for more than a twenty-minute drive. Now I'm about to get on the road for almost six hours. I'm "moving on."

"Okay, well . . . do you have everything?" Mom's eyes drift to the backseat, where the cooler of ready-made meals that she spent the last week preparing sits. I haven't exactly been eating well these past few months and she doesn't trust that I'll miraculously begin taking care of myself once I'm back in Lansing. Probably a safe bet.

"I'm good, Mom."

"How long before your new roommate gets there?"

"Next week." Derek's cousin, Rich, is coming back to Michigan State for his graduate degree. He texted me a few weeks ago, looking to rent Sasha's room. It took me eight days to respond but, in the end, I agreed to let him move in. I'm still not sure if that was a good idea, if having a complete stranger might not be better, but at least I won't be alone.

"Well, that's good. That'll give you some quiet time while you finish those exams. And take it easy with football practice."

"Yup." I avert my eyes. She's always been able to read a lie in them.

She leans in to give me a kiss on the forehead. "Call me when you get there." A pause and then, "Things will work out between you and Madison. Don't you worry."

My eyes drift to the "Sold" sticker crossing the sign on their front lawn. The Danielses' house sold in two days. Twenty-day closing. A bit fast, but I guess they just really want to get away. The next time I'm back here, a new family will have settled in nicely.

Mom steps back, giving my dad some room to maneuver his way in. He actually rescheduled his morning meetings to be here when I left. I haven't decided whether I think it's because he wants to say good-bye or because he doesn't believe I'll actually leave.

"You're doing the right thing, Cole. Heading back there, picking your life up again. You need to do this." With a pat on my shoulder, he steps back, sliding his hands into the pockets of his dress pants.

I pull away, the reflection of those two houses standing side-by-side in my rearview mirror.

The memory of children's laughter a hollow echo in my ears.

■ ■ ■

Almost four months vacant. I'm actually surprised no one broke into the apartment.

I let my duffel bag slide off my good shoulder. It hits the kitchen tile with a thud that echoes through the space. At eleven hundred square feet, it's a decent-sized place for two college guys. Right now, it feels too big.

Too empty.

We lucked out, grabbing the lease on the apartment from one of the seniors on our football team. We're ten minutes from campus and above a popular neighborhood pub. We've never minded the noise. The day Sasha and I picked up the keys, two years ago now, we weren't here for more than four hours before we threw a house-warming party. The night ended with noise complaints from neighboring houses and cops at our door, but luckily, no underage drinking charges.

Last year, the party was twice as big.

When my phone rings, I answer it without looking at the screen, expecting my mom. She has already called me three times on the way here.

"Did you make it?"

My heart starts racing at the sound of his voice. Then I put two and two together. "Rich?" I forgot that he sounds so much like Derek.

"Yeah, man! Listen, I was hoping to get the key off you tonight. Maybe we can grab a drink downstairs."

"Tonight?" I haven't seen Rich since the night of the accident. I also haven't touched a beer. I'm not ready for this. "Sure."

"'Kay. See you soon." I hang up the phone, the empty feeling in the pit of my stomach growing.

Hauling the rest of my things in takes no more than fifteen minutes and I'm left wandering the space, the emptiness screaming out so loud I can barely hear myself think. That's when I find myself standing over the big brown box that Susan Daniels gave me, small switchblade in hand. I've been staring at that box for over a week now, afraid to open it.

I slice open the clear tape that seals the contents—knowing I'll find as much of my childhood as Sasha's inside. A mishmash of things that I recognize well: A never-worn Notre Dame jersey that Sasha bought nine years ago, when Cyril and my dad took us down to a game. Ironic that we ended up playing for one of their rival teams. A well-used Xbox with every version of *Halo* ever made. I kicked Sasha's ass in every single one of them. He had to replace the controllers twice after whipping them against the wall in anger. A binder with his baseball card collection, including his prized Mickey Mantle card.

Beneath a bunch of ticket stubs from games and concerts that we had seen together—it's not so much that Sasha was a nostalgic guy as he just got into the habit of tossing those into his sock drawer—is a folded piece of paper.

When I open it up and find the four lines in a child's large print staring back at me, a chill rushes through me. I haven't seen this in years. Sasha, Derek, and I wrote the friendship pact in second grade, after I got pissed off at Sasha for lying about a doctor's appointment and ditching me to play with Derek. We didn't talk to each other for four days. An eternity, back then. When we finally made amends—thanks to the intervention of our mothers, who were tired of seeing their sons moping around every night after school—we made the pact.

> *Friends and brothers forever.*
> *We will never lie to each other.*
> *Your stuff is my stuff and my stuff is your stuff.*
> *We will never leave a man behind.*

Slightly dramatic, especially for three seven-year-olds. The words blur behind my unshed tears but I'm chuckling. That last line must have had something to do with the G.I. Joe comics we were obsessed with. The three brown stains on the bottom, where we jabbed ourselves with Susan's sewing needle and signed with our bloody fingerprints, added a nice touch.

The page slips from my fingers and floats down to land soundlessly in the box. I kick the box once, sending it sliding across the floor. And then I fall back onto the mattress, a wave of bitterness coursing through my veins.

I don't know if Sasha ever lied to me in the fourteen years in between, but I know he lied to me again three months ago, when he said he was fine to drive. When he held his hand out. I trusted him and he lied.

And they both sure as hell left me behind.

There's a loud knock against the front door. I contemplate not answering it, but it's probably Rich. At least I hope it's Rich. As much as I'm not ready for him, I'm definitely not ready to deal with any surprise guests.

The sight of him standing on my doorstep knocks the air out of my lungs.

"Hey." He bites his bottom lip as he holds out a hand, as if he's as uneasy about this reunion as I am.

When I offer him my right hand, he shakes it for one, two, three seconds, before I see a decision flicker through his eyes and he pulls me into him in a hug. "Good to see you again, man," he says, his voice suddenly husky.

I swallow against the flood of emotions that hits me and simply nod, backing up to give him some room.

He doesn't enter, though, his gaze drifting down the long hall. He came here with Derek before. It must be weird for him too. "How about we grab that drink? Looks like a happening Friday night downstairs."

I grab my keys from the hook by the door and follow him out without a word.

■ ■ ■

It took five pints for Rich to bring the accident up after mindless babble about everything *but* that night. "I still can't believe it happened. I had no idea you guys were heading out. If I had known, I would have stopped you. I swear."

I imagine that's the standard response anyone would give after hosting a party where a guest leaves drunk and kills five people plus himself. I could answer with, "If I had known Sasha was drunk, I wouldn't have given him the keys," but that sounds like an excuse. There are no excuses. So, I simply nod and take another long haul of my beer. I thought I was going to puke on the first one but, after choking it down, the rest have gone down too easy.

"I miss him. We had some good laughs growing up, me and Derek. Even though he was two years younger than me." Rich's blue eyes survey the young crowd, I'm guessing mainly students who decided to stay around and take summer classes. I recognize one or two faces but I avoid eye contact. Judging by their frequent glances over, they know who I am. "It sure stirred up a shitstorm in our family. It's been radio silence between my mom and my aunt for months now. She wanted to sue me for hosting the party. Luckily my uncle talked her out of that. I know she's just angry and hurt. Suing me isn't going to change anything."

"Yeah, it's crazy what people will do when they're grieving." Though my parents haven't said too much, I know that the parents of Billy, Kacey's boyfriend, are still looking to sue my dad for more money and my dad's looking to avoid that mess by settling out of court.

He waves down the waitress for another drink as he sets his beer down. "How are Sasha's parents doing? And your girlfriend?"

"They seem to be moving on. Madison and I are . . . taking a break." When I saw Madison loading her suitcase into her car, I went out to say good-bye. She crumbled in my arms all over again.

"Shit. How are you with that? With *all* of this?" I feel his gaze on me as I swish my beer around in my glass.

"You know." No. He doesn't. No one does, really.

"Well, I can tell you one thing for sure: it was one hell of a wake-up call for a lot of people around here. The newspapers were all over that story. Hey, what ever happened to that girl? The one who made it out?"

I shift in my seat, suddenly uncomfortable. "She's alive, the last I heard, but that's all I know. She won't let anyone near her."

"Yeah, that must have fucked her up bad. I saw the pictures of the car." He clears his throat roughly.

We shift back into idle chatter as a few of Rich's old friends swing by. Guys I don't know, who don't know me, thankfully.

They're football junkies. We talk about the coming NFL season and some dumb trades made by franchises. Nothing important. I mostly sit and listen, not interested in participating but less interested in sitting in my apartment alone. Though I'm beginning to hope that Rich will crash here tonight, seeing as he's going beer-for-beer with me.

Funny. I never really noticed that kind of thing before.

When the girl that Rich has been seeing shows up with her friend, I give them an obligatory smile and shift over in the booth to make room. By their infectious giggles and the way the girl mauls Rich's face, I'd say they've been enjoying a few drinks somewhere else tonight.

"Hey, I'm Monika." Sparkly-painted nails catch my eye as she holds out her hand.

"Cole."

She bats her lashes as she tests my name out on her tongue. "Cole . . . I like that name."

That makes one of us.

"Do you go to school here?"

"Does he go to school here? Don't you know this is Cole Reynolds, tight end for the Spartans?" Rich bellows, his girl-friend now perched on his lap.

Not anymore. "Shut it." I manage a half-smile as I toss a coaster at him. But I'm also holding my breath, waiting for this girl to recognize my name, to bring the accident up.

After a few long seconds, when she does nothing but giggle, I release it and let my body melt back into the bench. Maybe this is all I need. A few pints, a night out with a friend, some laughs. Maybe this will be the night that kick-starts my new life without my best friends.

■ ■ ■

What the fuck have I done?

I was drunk, but I remember every step that led to having this blond lying in my bed, tangled up in my sheets, leaving me buck naked and stretched out next to her. It wasn't because I thought she was particularly attractive. I just didn't want to be alone and she was convenient.

And more than willing.

I don't think I was even nice to her. What the hell is her name?

I stare out the window at the overcast sky, trying to dull the pounding ache between my eyes with thoughts of a red-haired girl. Wondering how she is.

Wondering if she feels like I do right now, like she'll never be free of that night. She must feel it. She's the only one who possibly could.

Maybe it's time I found out.

Chapter 7

As big as Grand Rapids is—almost twice the size of Lansing—I've never had any reason to visit the city before. As I face her door, a bunch of flowers gripped within my sweaty, shaking hands, I acknowledge that I still have no valid reason.

It wasn't that hard to find Kacey Cleary. It took visits to two hospitals and several inquiries, but finally I got a room number. I'm not sure what that says about our privacy laws, but right now I'm thankful for the nurse who doesn't seem to respect them.

With cautious steps, I close the distance, the taste of bile sitting in the back of my throat. I never used to hate hospitals. Now, that sterile smell overwhelms me, and each gurney that rolls by causes my back to tense.

I'm ready to turn around and run. What am I going to see behind that glass? Three months later, she's still here. Can she even get up? Is her body trapped in casting and a Frankenstein metal contraption?

Whatever athletic figure she had pre-accident must have wasted away by now. Is she a pile of skin and bones? Enough muscle to simply function and nothing more?

And that pretty face of hers . . . is she disfigured now?

I'm ten feet away and I can't will myself closer to the deeper, harsher stage of reality that I have yet to face. What will I even say?

Hi, I'm Cole. I was the guy who couldn't just not drink for a night, who didn't uphold his end of the deal to drive his friends home.

Hi, I'm the dumbass who handed the driver his keys, enabling him to kill your loved ones.

Hi. You're here because of me.

More than likely, I'll just step into her room and stand there, staring at her like an idiot, because there is nothing that I can say to make this better. In fact, I'll probably only make today even worse for her than it already is. I certainly won't get what I was coming here for. Why did I come again? Did I think this would somehow alleviate my guilt?

I still can't will myself forward.

When the door suddenly opens, my stomach drops. A girl with raven-black hair steps out. I recognize her immediately. Kacey's little sister, Olivia, who goes by "Livie."

She's crying.

All she has to do is look up and she'll see me. Will she know who I am?

She doesn't look up though. She simply rubs the tears away with the palm of her hand and then walks past, leaving me now dreading what's behind that door even more.

"Excuse me, can I help you?"

I jump at the voice, and turn to find a brown-haired nurse standing next to me. "Yeah, can you please put these in Kacey Cleary's room for me?" I shove the bouquet into her face, forcing her to accept them.

And then I get the hell out of there, heading in the opposite direction of Livie and anything to do with facing this nightmare.

■ ■ ■

A hundred or so beige seats stretch out in front of me. For as big as MSU is, with 47,000 students in attendance, many of my program classes are relegated to the same area. This will be my seventh time taking a class in this lecture hall. It's my first time sitting in the back row, though.

And it's definitely my first time consciously avoiding all eye contact.

I can feel them watching me. From glances over their shoulders to full-on stares, countless eyes full of everything from curiosity to judgment burn my skin.

They all know exactly who I am. Our program isn't that big, and given that I've spent three years with most of these people and I played for the Spartans, my name is known. My face is, too, based on the comments I've received over the years from the female student population.

But they're not looking at me for those reasons now, and so I keep my head down.

I smell her perfume a second before she slides into the seat beside me.

"Hi." It's a flat word, not genuine at all.

With a sigh, I turn to look at the brunette. "Hey." I recognize her but I have no idea what her name is.

By the set of her jaw, she looks like she's not here to introduce herself to me. She looks like she's on a mission.

"I knew Mr. Cleary. He was one of the nicest, funniest teachers I've ever had."

She pauses, as if waiting to see how I'll respond to that well-aimed verbal stab into my stomach. What the hell am I supposed to say? Especially with an audience. Even Professor Giles is now standing at attention by the podium, her attention focused on the back of her room when she should be starting the class.

Gritting my teeth, I manage, "I'm sure he was."

The girl opens her mouth to speak but then hesitates. She *must* see that she's already sufficiently wounded me, that the guilt is pouring from me in a constant stream. "He didn't deserve what you and your friends did to him. None of them did." With that, she gets out of the chair and heads toward the front of the lecture hall, her chin held high, having said her piece. I wonder if she's been planning that confrontation all summer long or if it was a spontaneous outburst.

"Welcome back, everyone!" Professor Giles calls out, pulling everyone's attention to the front.

Except mine. I quickly tune her out, dropping my gaze to the blur of words in my textbook. Why the fuck am I even here? When I chose Art History and Visual Culture as my area of study, I knew it was purely a stepping-stone. Truthfully, I could have skipped the degree and gone straight to a one-year design school program. I'd already be working full time at my mom's agency. But I wanted the full college experience—the parties, college ball, the piece of paper that should be coated in gold for what it cost. So did Sasha and Derek. Our parents weren't the least bit surprised when we applied to the exact same list of colleges and made our decision based on where all three of us had been accepted.

Now, though, I don't care about any of it.

Because *everything* has changed. Being here doesn't feel right anymore. It's like I'm trying to step back into the past and the door is firmly shut, with deadbolts barring it, the key thrown into a deep well.

I close my textbook and slip out the door, escaping the judgment.

■ ■ ■

"How'd it go?" Rich asks from the couch, one foot on the coffee table, one beer in hand.

I toss my empty knapsack on the floor. I returned my textbooks. All of them. "I'm out."

He sits up straight, a frown on his face. "What do you mean?"

"I mean I'm out." It took one more class of staring at pages and not hearing a single word spoken for me to make my decision. Though no one else decided to bludgeon my conscience, I felt the stares. I have a hard enough time living in my own skin right now. I can't deal with this.

Falling back into the couch beside him—even sitting on this couch is uncomfortable—I sigh. "Do you think you can find a roommate to take over my half of the rent?"

Rich's gaze burns into my profile for a long moment but I ignore it, gluing my eyes to the TV, zoning out on nothingness. "Yeah, for sure." Another long moment of silence. "You wanna beer? The fridge is loaded."

"Nope." I'm done with alcohol.

I'm done with this apartment.

With this school.

I'm done with everything.

■ ■ ■

"Hey! Can you get that for us?" The boy points to the bush at the end of my parents' driveway, where the hockey puck landed.

I retrieve it and toss it back onto the road. He and the other kid resume passing it back and forth between their hockey sticks without even a thanks my way.

Little shits. I smile. They're good. Not as good as Sasha and I were. The Danielses' front door opens and a brunette woman steps out. "Boys! Dinner." Of course they ignore her, too focused on the puck.

Slinging my duffel bag over my shoulder, I walk up the flagstone path to the unlit front porch. Our house is modest. My parents had talked about moving once, to a wealthier neighborhood in Rochester a good twenty minutes away from Sasha. I threw such a fit that they never talked about it ever again.

I find my parents sitting at the kitchen table, a tumblerful of amber liquid in my dad's hand, my mom's face full of resignation. Whatever they were talking about has created a tension in the air so thick that I feel like I'm walking into a fog. Ten bucks says it's about me.

"Cole?" My dad's brow tightens in a frown. "What are you doing here?"

I look to my mom when I say, "I needed to come home."

She nods slowly. I wonder if she expected this.

"You can't just walk away!" My dad yelling is such a rare sound, I have to wonder if he's graduated beyond one glass of scotch a night.

"I can't do it."

"You have one year left of your degree!"

Yeah, one unbearably long year. I know myself well enough to know that I'm not getting up for class tomorrow, or the next day, or the next day. "And then what? It's a fucking piece of paper."

"A piece of paper that we've paid for!" My dad slams his fist against the table.

"Carter!" My mom's yelling now too.

I knew there was a good chance I'd be facing this and yet I can't deal with it. I stroll out of the kitchen and head for my room, tossing my bag on the ground and flopping onto my bed, the feel of my cool pillow a relief.

A few minutes later, the door opens and shuts softly, and I know it's my mom without looking. "I just need to stay here for a while, until I can get back on my feet."

"I understand." A soothing hand lands on the back of my head.

"Can you throw me a few projects? Stuff I can work on from home. Alone."

"Yes. Okay."

"Thanks, Mom." I pause. "What were you and Dad talking about?"

She doesn't answer right away, and I can feel her choosing her words. "They need him in the Manhattan office. He's going to look into a place to rent, seeing as he's going to be there a lot."

"I thought he said he'd never do that." His partners have been trying to get him to move for years, but it was too big a risk to my mom's agency, and it's always been a rule for Carter Reynolds that he stays with his family.

I guess things have changed.

Chapter 8

December 31, 2008

"Hey, buddy! Glad you came." I throw a hand up in time to catch Fitz's friendly slap. "Beer?"

"Nah, I'm good. I can't stay long." My eyes survey the sea of familiar faces from high school. A lot of them I saw back in April at the funeral. That was eight months ago. They all look the same. With a full beard covering my face and at least twenty pounds less muscle, I'm sure they wouldn't say the same about me.

I'd still be sitting in my boxer shorts and T-shirt had my mom not run into Fitz's mom at the supermarket, who told her about the New Year's party that Fitz was throwing. My mom guilt-tripped me into coming.

I obliged, with the plan to show my face and then bolt.

"So . . . What have you been up to? I hear you're back in the neighborhood." I don't miss the way he shifts on his feet. He's probably as uncomfortable as I am right now.

"Uh . . . you know. Just work and stuff." It's as though I've forgotten how to carry on a normal conversation. I just don't know what to say to *anyone* anymore. That's why I rarely leave home. The rec room has become my lair. I've even moved my bed down. It's odd—I was always such an extrovert before, and rarely alone. But I can honestly say that I've come to appreciate the peace that solitude can provide. At least I can judge myself in privacy.

"All right, well . . ." Poor Fitz just wants to get away from me. "We've got burgers on the grill and the hockey game on in the living room. Help yourself to the stock in the fridge if you change your mind."

Another hand slap and then Fitz is out, his steps fast and heading in the opposite direction of me.

I glance at my watch, giving myself five minutes before the front door sees my back. Five long minutes to kill. Luckily, the place is crammed with people and the music is loud. It's easy to squeeze through the crowd with a nod and a smile without actually being forced to talk to anyone.

So, that's what I do, weaving through room after room. It's a big house, and Fitz's parents have always been cool about him throwing parties here. Even in high school, they'd take off for New York City, five hours and change away, and let him do whatever he wanted, as long as the house was spotless by the time they came back the next day.

I pass through the kitchen. And smile, remembering the beer bong showdown between Sasha and me at that very table in the corner. He won, of course, but it was—

Fuck. Just fucking stop, Cole.

Stop thinking about him.

Sasha's dead.

Gritting my teeth, I keep moving, into the living room where the Red Wings game is on.

And Madison is sitting on Henry's lap.

She stopped texting back in October, after I ignored countless attempts to reconnect and then sent her one single message, asking her to please stop. I figured it was best to just let her wounds heal, undisturbed by me. I guess they have. The Madison I know wouldn't be sitting on a guy's lap unless she was really into him.

She doesn't see me right away, giving me a chance to watch her for a moment, leaning into his chest, a cute smile touching her lips as he whispers something in her ear. Her head falls back and that boisterous laugh of hers that I always loved—way too big to fit into that tiny body—bursts out.

I'm beyond feeling pain over loss anymore, or I'm sure this would feel like a kick to the gut. Instead, a tiny smile touches my lips, such a foreign sensation to me now. She's moved on. Exactly what I told her to do.

I wish I could keep that smile for just a while longer, but when those whiskey-colored eyes—Sasha's eyes—suddenly land on me, and her face pales, the smile drops away.

I'm sure it's been five minutes by now. And if not? I don't really care anymore.

I'm out the door and halfway down the walkway when I hear her shout my name. She's running out in socked feet, her arms curled around her chest against the blistering cold. "I didn't think you'd be here. I'm . . . sorry."

She's apologizing to me. It's almost laughable. "You have nothing to be sorry about."

She searches my face for a long moment. "Still."

I attempt to lighten the awkwardness. "Henry always did have a thing for you."

A sheepish smile passes her lips. "Yeah, that's what he told me. I had no idea." Of course she didn't. Madison has no clue how beautiful and sweet she is. "How are you? My mom said you moved home?"

"Yup."

Her smile falls as she swallows hard and asks in a soft, sad voice, "How could you just cut me off like that?"

"I didn't want you to hold on to hope."

She nods, bowing her head until she can control the tears threatening. "Well . . . Happy birthday. I wanted to come by and drop a card or something off, but . . ." Her voice drifts. Madison has been there to celebrate my birthday for as long as I can remember, before *she* can even remember. First as friends, then as more.

Now as something lost.

I'll never be that guy again, and what we had is really and truly gone. The simple fact that she is able to move on creates an impassable rift between us, the connection we once shared growing more distant with each day.

"Have a happy new year, Mads." I turn and continue down the path, struggling to draw a breath, my lungs heavy.

It's suddenly so clear. The guy Madison loved died in a terrible car crash last April.

She deserves to be happy, and it'll never be with what was left behind.

Chapter 9

February 2009

I wake up to my dad's bellowing voice from the kitchen. "Why am I hearing about this from a goddamn newspaper!"

I knew this was going to happen.

I can picture him sitting, leg crossed, mug of coffee steaming, the kitchen table covered with a myriad of papers. That's how he's always spent his Saturday mornings. I'm glad to see that at least one thing hasn't changed.

He's seen the notice that the courts made me publish in the local paper, after I filed my petition for my name change. Because now that I've realized that Cole Reynolds is dead, there's no need to keep answering for him anymore.

I roll out of bed, pulling on a pair of track pants on my way out the door. I guess I could have warned him. But what's the point? I knew he wouldn't agree to it. My mom knows. It took less convincing than I expected. Maybe that's because I'm using my middle name and her maiden name. Or maybe it's because she doesn't know how to handle me.

I can't hear my mom's response but whatever it is, my dad's not happy about it. "Supporting him with this isn't helping him, Bonnie! He needs to deal with what happened and move on!" my dad yells as I round the corner.

"I am. Dealing with it, I mean."

They both stop to turn and look at me. My dad's wearing dress pants and a button-down shirt, as if he's heading out somewhere. He hasn't been home in weeks, and yet I see his bags sitting in the corner. He's ready to leave again. I'm starting to wonder if it's more about the office expansion or about the bits of conversations I've overheard, comments about the lawsuit from the family of that guy, Billy, and the partners not being happy with all the billing hours they're burning, and how they're worried that this case will look bad for the firm if clients catch wind.

I don't know how true that is, but just the possibility weighs on me.

"By becoming *Trent Emerson*?" My dad throws the paper to the floor.

"By letting go of who I was." I swiftly pick it up and tuck it under my arm. Proof for the court so they can finalize my petition.

I almost miss the head shake, it's so subtle. "What does your therapist say about this?"

I stall with my tongue sliding over my teeth, deciding how I want to answer that. Is now a good time to tell him that I stopped going back in October, after four two-hundred-dollar sessions of the guy asking me how I feel and me telling him that I feel damn guilty and getting nowhere beyond that?

Another thing my mother knows that we haven't enlightened my dad about.

But he's smart enough to figure it out on his own, it would seem. He throws his hands up in exasperation. "I don't know what to do anymore, Cole. Please! Tell me how we can help you. Everyone else is putting their life back together and yet you don't seem at all interested in helping yourself." His tone, his words, the way he's looking at me—all of it is sliding beneath my skin.

"I'm not discussing this decision. It's mine to make and I've made it."

"But this is crazy!" The confusion in his eyes is genuine. "You can't move on by doing this, and you *need* to move on!"

"I don't deserve to!" I bellow. My dad flinches with surprise. I can't remember the last time I yelled at him like that, if ever, but I don't stop now. He doesn't get it. No one gets it, and they need to. "Why should I get to move on? Sasha and Derek can't! Kacey Cleary can't!" I've found myself thinking about her more than I do Sasha and Derek lately. I haven't stopped thinking about her. Every day, from the moment I open my eyes to the moment I drift off to oblivion, I can feel her shadow haunting my subconscious. She was so completely innocent in all of this.

It probably doesn't help that I've saved a picture of her onto my phone and I check it at least ten times a day—every time I imagine a new way that she may be disfigured and I'm desperate to bleach the image from my mind I fixate on her photo. On her smile.

Only it's cyclic, because then I remember that that smile has surely been wiped away. By me. And I'm not even brave enough to face her in the hospital, to confess to my part in it. To say I'm so damn sorry. That I'd do anything to fix it.

I don't remember what it's like to *not* feel this toxic mixture anymore—pain and sadness and guilt that eats away at my insides, leaving me hollow and wishing that I could just lay my head on my pillow one night and never have to lift it off again.

"Kacey Cleary will be released soon—" my dad begins to say, but I cut him off.

"To what? She has no one left! They're all dead because of me!" The paper I just picked up goes flying across the room, hitting a glass that sits on the counter, knocking it to the ground, to shatter into countless pieces. "So how am I supposed to just move on? Please explain that to me, Dad! How? I'm just going to finish my degree and play ball and laugh and *live*? I don't deserve to *live*! Don't you two see that?" The words tumble out of my mouth, more than I've said in almost a year, more than I've admitted to anyone.

They seem to deflate my dad. The anger and frustration that contorted his face before slides off, leaving only a tired, wary man who falls into his chair, as if his legs can't hold the weight of him anymore as his hope for his only son falls to the kitchen floor, to lie with the shattered glass.

A heavy silence hangs over us.

"You're right, Sasha and Derek can't," my mom says shakily, stepping forward to take my hands. "But you can and we need you to. *Please*. For us. For everyone who loves you. For yourself." Her eyes are watering. I've never seen my mom cry as much as I have in the last ten months. Hell, *I've* never cried as much as I have in the last ten months. And seeing my parents like this now, *again*—like they're grasping at every last fiber that's keeping them together, like they're about to unwind into a heap—deflates whatever fight I have left. "We love you, Cole. And we miss you. *Please*." Her pleas turn into whispers. "I need my son back."

I bow my head to avoid facing her pain. I've hurt so many people and I'm *still* doing it. I'm hurting my parents so much. I know it every time I look into their eyes.

"Yeah, Mom. I'll try."

For all that it's worth.

Chapter 10

August 2009

"Any more boxes?" my dad asks.

"I've got it. I'll meet you outside," I holler back, the yellow folder staring up at me.

I should have known. Being the astute lawyer that he is, my dad has a file of information on the Cleary family. Notes about their ages, schools, the date that Kacey was released from the rehabilitation center. The address of her aunt and uncle's, where she and her little sister now live. Where her parents are buried.

Her medical bills.

So many medical bills, which my parents are obviously taking care of.

Billy's family settled with my parents out of court, for how much I can't say, because neither of them will tell me. But I doubt they'll be able to buy that summer home on the Cape anymore, and that guilt festers inside me.

It's a complete fluke that I've come across this information. I opened the box with the intention of dividing the files into two boxes, because I knew there was no way my dad would be able to lift it. The Cleary name was right there, waiting for me.

I check over my shoulder to make sure he's not at the door, watching me. I wish I had time to make copies of everything, but I don't. So I do the next best thing. Pulling my phone out, I take pictures of all the most important information.

My dad's waiting for me by his replacement Suburban,

the back fully loaded. Mainly with office stuff and sentimental things. Most of his belongings are already at his place in New York—a semi-detached house in Astoria that he's been renting for almost a year.

The place he will now call home.

The high school sweethearts voted most likely to grow old together have decided that they need time and space from each other, and the life they once seemed to cherish.

I still haven't gotten more than a vague answer from either of them about why. Which makes me pretty certain that I know what the reason is.

I eye the loaded trunk. "You sure you don't need my help on the other end?"

My dad slaps my bicep—my arms now bigger and stronger than they ever were during my years of college ball, thanks to all of the hours I spend at the gym. "I may be old, but I can handle a few boxes of books."

"Right." I give him a half-smirk. It's the best I can manage but he seems happy to see it, chuckling to himself. Though still strained, our relationship is better than it has been in a while.

"Okay, well . . . You keep your mom in line here. I know she was talking about maybe taking a vacation or something. Just"— his eyes drift to the walkway, to the front door, where Bonnie Reynolds leans against the doorframe, her lips pressed into a firm line, watching—"keep up with your courses and work and . . . getting your life back on track."

Back on track.

Do they *really* believe that that's what I'm doing? I suppose I've been successful at making it look like I am. I've put up a good front, learning how to force smiles and appear reserved versus emotionally unstable. I ask polite questions. The trick is to ask open-ended ones that force others to talk. And then just keep asking questions. That way they think you're having a conversation. It's hard and tiring, because my mind keeps drifting.

I've also made myself look busy. I kill my mornings on mindless graphic design program courses, my afternoons on undemanding design projects from my mom, my evenings at the local gym, and long hours sleeping and thinking about the red-haired girl that I don't have the guts to face, before I hit repeat. One never-ending stream.

I threw the rhythm off just twice: once, on the one-year anniversary of the car accident. That day I sat in the cemetery with a fifth of Jack Daniel's, babbling to Sasha's tombstone; the second time was to appease my mother and go on a blind date that Fitz set me up on. A friend of his sister's. Nice enough girl, but I think she was going in with the impression that she could turn my life around. For about four minutes, while I fucked her in the backseat of my car, I thought maybe she could too. Then reality came crashing down with a vengeance. I haven't called her since.

I'm better off sticking to my simple schedule. A schedule that doesn't allow me to let any of this go, but at least gives me something to focus on while I burn time. Just waiting for the knots in my stomach and the hollowness in my chest to go away.

Just waiting until I can be like everyone else, and move on.

Well, maybe not everyone.

Has Kacey moved on too, yet?

"A change of scenery may be good for you. You should come visit me sometime, Cole."

I grit my teeth at the name. That's one of the reasons I spend so much time at the gym. I'm only Trent Emerson there.

My dad must see my reaction. He opens his mouth but hesitates. He ends with, "Think about it."

And then I watch my dad officially separate from my mom after twenty-five years of marriage.

Chapter 11

February 2010

"Come on! It'll be a good time." Rich slaps my back as we climb a set of stairs that I didn't think I'd ever be climbing again. The big house looks exactly the same—colorful flags plastering the walls, kegs lining the entranceway, drunk freshmen looking to hook up. Sasha, Derek, and I experienced our first MSU frat party within these very walls. And the front lawn . . . well, Derek later painted *that* with too many shots of Fireball.

"We're too old for this." I pull my baseball cap down lower. Though there are a few upper years here, and of course the frat brothers, at twenty-two and with my solid frame, I stand out.

"No, *I'm* too old for this. You're borderline."

I can't believe I'm back here. I can't believe I'm crashing in my old room, now vacant again. It feels both like no time and an eternity have passed, the wounds that never healed somehow torn wide open. But I'm numb to the fresh wave of pain because I haven't felt anything but that in almost two years.

Rich phoned me two weeks ago and begged me to come out to visit. My mom overheard and interpreted the conversation, and then prodded me until I agreed. I can see now that I should have just dug my heels in, but I do pretty much whatever my mother asks me to. It keeps her happy.

Thirty seconds in the door and I'm already exhausted. I'm used to solitude now. Not two hundred freshmen bumping into me from all sides. Something I would never have noticed when I was drunk but that irritates the shit out of me now that I'm sober. Luckily, I can see over the sea of heads.

That's how I spot her.

There's no doubt that it's her; I've memorized her face.

Leaning against a wall on the opposite side, her lips wrapped around a clear bottle filled with clear liquor, her fiery red hair a wild mane against the stark white wall, a tight black T-shirt showing off toned arms. She's in no rush to part with that bottle, guzzling back a good portion before she hands it off to someone, wiping her mouth with the back of her hand.

Her eyes at half-mast.

She's wasted.

My heart starts racing. What the hell is Kacey Cleary doing here? By my calculation, she's probably finishing her last year of high school, having lost at least half a year while recovering.

I tug my cap down even farther, though I doubt she can see two feet in front of her.

Shit. What if she does recognize me? How would she react? Does she know my real name? What I look like? I can't say for sure that my face wasn't printed in a newspaper somewhere. She could have Googled my name and found a dozen game shots with me in them. I have my helmet on in most of them, but you can find a profile picture of me easily enough if you're looking.

I don't know that she was, though. I wonder if Kacey Cleary gives a fuck about anything anymore. Her Facebook account is inactive. She hasn't posted a single word and the well-wishes have dwindled, as everyone moves on.

I do know that she shouldn't be at a party in this state. I've heard of bad things happening when girls get that drunk. Especially when they don't care.

But what do I do?

A blond stumbles into my chest with two beers in hand.

"Hey, do you go here? What's your name?" She's tipping her head back way farther than necessary to look up at me, telling me she's trying to flirt but is too drunk to do it right.

I smile down at her anyway. She's a good cover. I can stand right here and watch Kacey. "I'm Trent, and I used to go here."

"Really? When'd you graduate?"

From the corner of my eye, I see Kacey shift from the wall and begin climbing the stairs, her arm hooked around the railing to help her. Two guys following her.

Shit. "Uh . . . two years ago."

"Cool. I'm Kimmy, by the way. Here." She shoves the beer toward me, splashing some onto my chest.

Just what I want. To smell like a brewery. I take it anyway, because you just don't come to a keg party and *not* drink. I suffer through another few minutes of conversation, worrying about where Kacey went and what's going on, when Kimmy asks, "So, who did you come here with?"

Perfect. My out. Rich has disappeared into the crowd. He's like his cousin—a social butterfly. "A friend. Actually, if you don't mind, I need to go find him." I flash her a smile. No reason to be a dick to her. "It was nice talking to you, Kimmy."

I don't wait for her response before I push my way through the crowd to the stairs, my pace picking up with each step. "Where'd the redhead go?" I ask the guys leaning against the railing at the top of the landing, waiting in line for the can. A head nod directs me to the closed door at the end of the hall.

The *locked*, closed door.

I start hammering against it with my fist.

I can just make out a male voice hollering, "Busy!" from inside.

"Open the damn door. She needs to get home. *Now.*" It's a risky move. I don't know how she's going to react to any of this.

I half-expect her to throw the door open herself and tell me to fuck off. But when she doesn't, I start hammering against the door again. I've earned a small audience by now but I don't care. "You've got exactly ten seconds before I bust this door down!" And I can. Easily. I'll probably end up with a dozen frat guys jumping onto my back, too, but oh well.

"Whoa! Wait up!" someone yells behind me. A dark-haired guy steps in beside me. "Cole?"

It takes me a moment to recognize him. "Vance. Right?" A fellow Spartan who joined the team two years after me.

"Yeah." He flashes a crooked smile. "How've you been?"

I brush his question off. "I need to get this girl out. She's not up for whatever's going on in there."

He starts banging on the door. "Griff. Open up! It's Vance."

There's a long pause, and then I see the handle jiggle.

"Hey!" a guy hollers as I barrel into him, pushing my way through and into the room.

To find Kacey lying on the bed in her black bra and panties, her jeans hanging off one leg. Unconscious. Or close to it, with her eyes shut, her limbs lax, her lips moving ever so feebly.

And *two* assholes in the room with her. Ready to do God knows what.

Rage ignites in me and I lunge for the guy closest to me, the one who opened the door. The one with his shirt off and his belt undone. Vance jumps in between to stop me, but I send him flying with ease. "What the hell is she on? Did you slip her something?"

"No! Nothing! She was into it five minutes ago." The guy's hands fly up in surrender, fear touching his eyes as I seize his shirt. "She grabbed both of us and said she wanted it. But now she's like *that*. We weren't gonna do anything to her."

"Right."

A crowd has gathered by the door. I kick the door shut in their faces.

Vance has regained his footing and steps in between again, along with the third guy. "Look, everyone's been drinking. Let's not get out of hand here." I know that's directed at me. We may have played ball together but these guys are obviously his buddies, and he's going to defend them no matter what. He juts his chin toward Kacey. "You know her?"

"Yeah." After staring at her picture every day for almost two years, I can honestly say that I do know her. I know the curve of her slender nose. I know the kaleidoscopic pattern of her pale blue irises. I know how, when she smiles, it's slightly crooked, earning a deeper dimple on the left side. I know the minuscule scar at her right temple.

"'Kay. Can you get her out of here?"

A wave of nausea hits me. Am I really going to do this? "Yup." I know where she lives.

He hesitates. "You good to drive, man?"

My glare answers.

In seconds, I'm alone in a room with Kacey Cleary.

And I need to remind myself how to breathe.

She's here, lying on the bed right in front of me, in a drug- and alcohol-induced unconsciousness. How often does she do this?

I don't know if those guys were telling the truth or not, but I'm sure she's been in other situations like this. And I'm also sure there was no one there to stop it. Even now, though I know it's wrong, I can't help but look at her face, at her body, as chiseled and beautiful as it is.

Even with countless thin surgical white scars running along the right side of her body. From her shoulder, down her arm, across her ribs, her waist, her hips, disappearing behind a flock of black ravens tattooed on her thigh. Ravens symbolize death; I know because my grandfather was highly superstitious and used to shake his fist at any raven that flew by.

There are one . . . two . . . three . . . four of them on her creamy pale skin. Four ravens for the four people in her life that died that night, maybe? No, wait . . . A black tip peeks out from where the top of her jeans sit on her right leg. I nudge them down with a finger.

A fifth raven.

Five ravens.

There were five in her car.

A chill runs down my back as I peer down at my fellow survivor. Maybe she didn't truly make it out of that car alive either.

Her eyes flicker open and I suck in my breath. "Youuuuu," she murmurs softly, and her lips fall back into an intoxicated smirk. A second of panic hits me, but then her eyes start rolling around. She can't even focus on me. There's no way she recognizes me.

How much did she drink? Enough to poison her blood-stream? Definitely enough that she may be puking within the hour. I don't really want that to start here.

With shaky hands, I crouch down to slip the loose pant leg over her foot.

She pulls it away with a small moan. "Come on . . . what's taking so long," she says in garbled speech, her lips barely moving. I'm surprised I can even understand it. Her hands slide across her taut belly and pelvis.

And she begins pushing her black panties down.

"Jesus! No." I dive for her hands to stop them from going any farther and shut my eyes, my heart nearly exploding in my chest. Wouldn't this be a sight for anyone walking in, after the trouble I gave those two idiots!

She shakes her hands away from mine with surprising force,

allowing me a chance to slide her panties back up. She doesn't fight me anymore as I manage to get her leg back into her jeans and tug them up over her hips. Finding her shirt on the floor, I work it over her head and then reach for her hand to guide it into the sleeve.

She jerks it away. "No . . . no . . . no . . ."

"I need to get your shirt on, Kacey," I whisper, reaching for her hand once again.

"No!" It's a bellow now, from deep within her. Her hand flies from mine once again. "No hands . . . No hands . . . No hands . . ." Over and over again, her distress rising.

"Okay! Okay. No hands," I promise, frowning. What is that about?

It's not easy, but I manage to get her shirt on. Slipping my arms beneath her knees and around her shoulders, I move to lift her up.

A slight giggle slips from her lips, and her eyes flicker open again. Freezing me. Even bloodshot and unfocused, they're gorgeous and light and hypnotizing. I can't peel myself away from them.

That's probably why she manages to get her hand coiled around my head and my mouth against hers before I know what the hell is going on. Her tongue, surprisingly responsive for someone as wrecked as she is, tangles itself with mine, drawing me in with unspoken promises, sending blood rushing through my veins.

It's all so unexpected, so fast, so fierce, that I can't stop it from happening. And then, as she wiggles within my grip and pulls me into her thighs, as her hands slide up the back of my shirt, I find that I don't want to stop it from happening. We could get lost here together, tumbling down this rabbit hole of blind emotion, in search of a desperate escape that we both want. And maybe that only the two of us can truly understand.

That's the precise moment when I come to grips with how low I've sunk.

"I can't . . ." I wrench myself away, a new kind of guilt growing inside. A disgusting, loathsome sickness in the pit of my stomach.

Adjusting my clothes and the hard-on that hasn't withered yet, despite my consciousness, I scoop her up again. Whatever brief spurt of energy she tapped into has faded, leaving her limp in my arms, her eyes closed.

"Did you come here with anyone?" I whisper more to myself, moving quickly and quietly down the stairs and through the crowd. I have no fucking clue what I'll say if anyone stops me.

But no one does.

Not one person—not one friend—stops me as I carry a semi-unconscious Kacey Cleary out of a party and into a cold winter's night in nothing but a T-shirt and jeans.

Doesn't she have *anyone* looking out for her?

She doesn't say another word until I sit her in the passenger seat of my car. "No . . . car . . . hate . . . car," she moans, making a feeble effort to roll out.

"Shhh . . . Kacey. I know." I brush her hair off her face. It's even softer than I imagined. "I get it. Just go to sleep." I hesitate before leaning in to recline the seat for her, wondering if she'll kiss me again.

Wondering if I'd let her.

Yes. I would. It's so wrong, and yet I would. What the fuck is my problem?

"It'll be okay," I promise, slipping her seat belt over her. Two years ago, I would have laid her down across the backseat and said screw the seat belt. But that's never happening again.

"I wish I could take you back to my apartment. It's so much closer," I mumble, tucking my coat over her body. Cranking the engine, I program her address—the one I saved in my phone—

into the GPS and pull my car away from the curb, not feeling the cold. Not feeling anything but shock over tonight's turn of events. What if I hadn't been there? What would have happened to her?

"Is this the real you? Or just the real you, now?" I whisper, turning to look at her. For everything else that happened to her, she has no glaring scars on her face. It's still beautiful. That's something, at least.

"Can you hear me? Kacey?" I can't stop saying her name.

No answer.

With hesitation, I reach out and graze her fingertips with mine. Not a moan, not a flinch.

So, I slip my fingers within hers, feeling the softness of her skin.

And I say the things I've wanted to say for so long. "I'm *so sorry*. For everything. If I could take it back, could change it, I would. I swear it. I'd trade my life in a heartbeat." And I would, honestly.

Somehow, saying these words doesn't make me feel better. Not even slightly. So I shut up for the remainder of the drive. It takes exactly fifty-eight minutes to reach Kacey's house, and I do it with the heat blasting and the radio silent, and holding Kacey Cleary's limp hand in mine.

She lives in a modest brick bungalow, with small, weathered windows and concrete steps leading up to a two-person porch. A dim light flickers, providing poor lighting for anyone coming home this late at night. The roof's been replaced and there's a new blue Camry parked in the driveway.

I let go of Kacey's hand to shake her shoulder gently. But she's not waking up. With a sigh, I pull forward until I'm two houses down.

And simply stare at this unconscious girl in my car. How am I going to keep track of her? How can I know this won't happen again? Right now, I wish I lived in Lansing. I'm too far away from her. Too far away to witness her deteriorate.

Before I can stop myself, and with careful hands, I search her pockets until my fingers wrap around her phone. No password to lock it down. I guess she doesn't care about someone stealing it. Or some creep invading her privacy.

Like I'm doing right now.

I quickly scroll through her screens, copying down her phone number.

The little email icon stares back at me. I scribble her email address down, too—just in case—and then I tuck her phone back into her pocket.

Scooping her up, I carry her up the sidewalk, up the worn pathway, up the stairs, to the tiny porch, watching for any late-night witnesses. Though no one's out at this time of night in the middle of winter.

"I'm going to put you down here," I whisper, setting her down on the concrete floor with reluctance, leaning her up against the brick wall. She hasn't stirred, hasn't moaned, hasn't cracked an eyelid. I wonder what the hell she's on.

And then I remember that I'm on her front porch, and the last thing I want is for her family to catch me here and begin asking questions. So I ring the doorbell and cross my fingers, my heart pounding the entire time.

Footsteps approach from inside about thirty seconds later. I leap over the railing to duck behind a tree about ten feet away, making it just as the storm door creaks open and her little sister appears, shielding her eyes against the bright light. "Kacey." She sighs. I was expecting a shriek, a cry. Something to tell me that this isn't common. "Why do you keep doing this to yourself?" The pain within the whisper is unmistakable. She bends down and places two fingers against her sister's wrist.

Because that's what it has come to for this thirteen-year-old.

Their aunt's head pops out—full of curlers, like you'd imagine seeing on an elderly woman. "How did she get here?" She squints into the darkness, searching, and I instinctively shrink back.

Livie's head is shaking before the words come out. "Can you help me with her?"

I have to root my feet to the ground to keep from stepping out from the shadows and carrying her in. No good will come of me storming into Kacey's life like this.

So, I watch a girl in Snoopy pajamas and a petite woman nearing her fifties try to drag a comatose Kacey into the house. It's futile. As slender as she is, she's pure muscle. Finally, after a few minutes, a groggy uncle in plaid flannel steps out and lifts her up.

"Come inside, Livie. It's freezing," the aunt calls out.

"In a minute," Livie says over her shoulder as the storm door shuts. Wrapping her arms tight around her body, she drops her head back and gazes at the stars in the clear night sky. It's dead quiet—so quiet that I'm afraid to move a muscle. "Please don't let me lose her too," she whispers to no one. Or maybe to someone. To two people she's already lost. She brushes her hand against her cheeks, wiping away the tears that have begun falling.

And the weight of what I've done to these girls truly hits me.

Kacey's spiraling. Just like me.

Chapter 12

April 2010

The streetlights flicker on and off as I wait, huddled in the cold. I've been parked out on the street for hours, slouched over in my seat, wary of her neighbors. The last thing I need is a call in to the cops about a strange guy lurking.

In that time, I've seen the aunt, a mousy woman with black hair and a buttoned-up blouse, come home from grocery shopping. I've seen Livie stroll past my car with a book bag slung off her shoulder and trudge up the stairs. I've seen the uncle drag his feet up the steps as if his construction boots are made of bricks, a brown liquor bag in hand.

But I haven't seen Kacey yet.

And it's eleven o'clock at night.

Granted she's eighteen, but still.

Two hours later, when the porch light is shut off and I start to think she may not have left the house to begin with, a red Dodge Spirit pulls up to the curb. The sight of her long, fiery red hair as she climbs out of the passenger side lightning-fast, like she couldn't wait to get out of the car, has me hunching into my seat.

She takes long, even strides toward the path up to her house, the hems of her jeans just barely dragging the ground.

"Hey!" a guy calls out.

Thanks to my cracked window, I hear her mutter a "fuck off."

A guy in ripped jeans and a chain hanging from his pocket steps out of the driver's side. "Hey!" he hollers again.

I hold my breath as she spins on the heels of her Converse sneakers and snaps, "What?"

He lifts his arm, a jacket and a plain black backpack dangling from his fingertips. "You forgot your stuff."

She wanders back reluctantly, holding her arms out. The streetlight casts just the right amount of light to show the white lines running along her toned arm. And the vacant stare in her watery blue eyes.

The sparkle is long gone.

"You just wanted to see me again, didn't you?" I can only see the guy's profile, but I don't like the leery smile that he's showing her. He probably has no clue that the sparkle is gone. He probably doesn't even care.

Snatching her bag and jacket from his grip, she blows a strand of fallen hair from her face. "Look . . . what was your name again? Rick? . . . Dick?"

"Mick," he answers dryly.

"Right, *Mick*. Well, *clearly* you were memorable." She oozes sarcasm. With that, she turns away.

He throws his hands up. "Seriously? Is that it?"

"What! We burned through a couple of lines and a couple of condoms. To be honest, the former was more enjoyable."

The guy honestly looks stunned. "You're a bitch."

My hands tighten around my steering wheel and I have to remind myself that I'm not supposed to be here.

If she's bothered by his words, she doesn't let on, plastering a fake, sickly sweet smile onto her lips. "Oh, I'm sorry. Are you in love with me now? Do you want to hold hands and talk about our future? Should we meet your parents? You can't meet mine, sorry. Though I'm sure they wouldn't approve of you, anyways. How about china patterns for the wedding?"

The guy stares at her like she's lost her mind.

"You should probably get in your car and drive away now." She turns toward the house again.

"I know what happened to you."

"You don't know shit," she throws back.

"Look, I'm sorry. Maybe next time we can go out and, I don't know . . ." He scratches the back of his head. "See a movie or something." I don't know if the guy's an asshole or not. If he's doing lines and then screwing around with her, he's definitely not a real catch. But right now he seems to be trying to appeal to her softer side.

"I'm not interested in movies or dinner or long walks on the beach. I'm not interested in friends. I'm not interested in getting to know you, or anyone else. And I sure as hell don't want to talk. So do me a favor, and get into your little car and drive away. Forget about me. I've already forgotten about you." She disappears into the house, the storm door slapping noisily against the frame.

Leaving me staring at the back of the Dodge Spirit, the hollowness inside me somehow growing. This isn't the real her. It can't be.

"Is there a reason you're sitting out here?" a voice beside my window asks, startling me enough that I jump. *Shit.* I didn't even notice the middle-aged man walking on the sidewalk and now he's staring at me, his eyes full of suspicion. A Great Dane tugs at his arm, wanting to continue on its walk.

I hold up my phone. "Had to take a call. Turned out to be a bad one and I needed to get my bearings."

The man's face softens. "Got it. Sorry, just noticed you here on my way out and, you know, we keep an eye on the neighborhood."

"Of course. Didn't mean to scare you." I crank the engine. He continues on his late-night dog walk, and I pull away.

Meanwhile, Kacey's completely lost.

Chapter 13

April 25, 2010

The puck sails into the net with fifteen seconds left in the second period, sending the stadium into a frenzy.

My dad slaps my back—just like he always does when the team we're cheering for scores a goal. Except this time, we're at Madison Square Garden, watching the game live. "I'm going to run to the restroom before the intermission."

I watch him weave his way up the concrete steps, noticing that the gray at his temples has spread. The last two years seem to have aged him faster than the ten before.

"He arm-wrestled Tesky in my office for your tickets," one of my dad's firm partners, Rolans, calls out from beside me.

"Was he in his suit?" A mental image of my dad, fists locked with the law firm's token partner—a seventy-five-year-old man who no longer takes cases and simply "counsels" and collects earnings—makes me smirk.

"Sleeves rolled up," Rolans confirms, adding more somberly, "he almost lost."

"No."

"Yeah, I'm serious." By the look on Rolans's face, I instantly know he's telling the truth. "Your dad's worn out. We've tried to force him to take a vacation, but he refuses. The billable hours he's putting in are fantastic, but they're going to kill him. This lawsuit is going to—"

"What lawsuit?" I interrupt.

"The one from your *accident*." He emphasizes that last word in a way that makes me think he has a distinct opinion about it. One that's not favorable toward me.

"The Turner family? I thought that was settled out of court."

"No, the Monroes. You know, the teenage girl who died?"

I feel my face screw up. I didn't even know they were suing.

"They're going after your dad for more money and he feels guilty enough to pay out. If you had any idea how much he's already lost in this . . ." Rolans shakes his head, his eyes trailing the Zamboni as it cleans the ice.

"How long has that been going on?" How long has he hidden it from me?

"A while."

"But the accident was two years ago."

He glances over at his daughter, April, whose focus is glued to her phone screen, as any typical fourteen-year-old's would be. "When you lose a kid, two years is nothing. Those parents will be missing their daughter for the next fifty years." Rolans's eyes flicker behind me, warning me that my dad is back before he takes his seat, ending all conversation.

The third period begins.

But in my head, it's already over.

■ ■ ■

"Good game, right?" my dad hollers from the kitchen.

I don't answer, simply taking in the wall of pictures. A shrine to our family. Some I recognize from the living room wall of the house my parents shared. Some must have been dug up from the shoe boxes my mom kept under her bed. The three of us together, my dad and me at hockey and football practice, my mom and me on the beach. Sasha and me in the backyard. My parents' wedding photos.

The full bottle of Johnnie Walker that sat on the bookshelf three nights ago when I arrived at his house in Astoria now sits half-empty. I guess leaving my mom didn't break him of his new-found vice. In fact, I think it has only amplified it. For a guy who preaches letting go and moving on, he sure as hell doesn't seem to be following his own advice.

"I had to fight Tesky to get those tickets," he jokes, stepping into the room, a glass of scotch against his lips. "It's not often a client hands us box seats to a play-off game, no matter how much they say they like the firm."

"I haven't seen a Rangers game in years," I acknowledge.

"Yeah, I think you were fifteen or so, the last time?" Scratching his stubbly chin in thought, he murmurs, "I can't believe how fast the time has flown."

Fast, and yet painstakingly slow. Two years ago, today, I was sitting on a couch in Rich's house, pounding beers. In a month, I can say my parents have been separated for a year. They just filed for divorce. Rolans is right. My dad has lost so much, and not just the money.

"You still love her, don't you?"

My dad sidles up beside me, settling his eyes—eyes I inherited—on a grainy old picture of my mom at sixteen, sitting on a set of wooden steps that lead to the public beach on the Cape, where they first met. I've heard the story a thousand times. My dad was tossing a Frisbee to his brother and my mom—oblivious—walked straight in between the two of them and took it in the head. And then she just started to laugh.

"I'll always love your mother."

"Can't you work it out? *Things* are . . . better now, aren't they?" There's nothing about what goes on in my head and heart on a daily basis that could be considered better.

"I guess our marriage finally faced a test that it couldn't pass," is all he finally says.

A car honk sounds outside. "That's my taxi. I'm going to head into the office for an hour or two to finish up some work. If you're fine with that."

The last time I glanced at the clock above the TV, it was almost eleven. On a Sunday night. When I haven't seen him since Christmas. I'm tempted to ask him about the lawsuit, but I don't. I simply nod as the door swings shut behind me.

I wonder if this is about those billable hours, making up all that he's lost for the firm and for himself. Or maybe he's simply drowning his sorrows over my mom in work. Or maybe he wants to get away from me for a while. There's no doubt that my dad loves me. But he's also got pictures on his wall of three little boys' smiling faces, their arms roped around each other's waists. I don't know a lot of dads who would include his son's friends on his bachelor pad wall.

Unless his son's friends were like second sons to him.

I reach for the bottle of scotch.

■ ■ ■

A soft ballad over the radio mixes with the low purr of the engine to create a soothing ambiance in my dad's crammed single-car garage. I let the darkness envelop me, my dashboard a blurry haze of green lines.

Her smile shining brightly up at me from the screen on my phone as I hit "call."

She answers on the third ring, shouting a "Hello?" into the receiver above the loud laughter and music on the other end. She must be at another party.

I close my eyes and cherish these few seconds connected to

her, as I did the other three times I called. I had my number blocked so she can't read my name—not that Trent Emerson would mean anything to her.

"Who the hell is this?"

I really should stop doing this, or else she'll change her number.

Not that it matters anymore.

"Listen, you creeper . . ."

Is she drunk? I think I detect a slur. But maybe it's just me who's drunk. And, *damn*, I am fucking loaded. I can't even focus on the steering wheel in front of me. But I have to say it. Just once, when she'll hear it, even if she doesn't remember tomorrow. "I'm sorry."

There's a long pause. "For what?"

I open my mouth but I can't bring myself to say the words, and so I say nothing.

"Drop dead, you douchebag." The phone clicks.

It has taken almost two years and the half bottle of scotch that I just downed, but everything is suddenly so obvious.

I wasn't meant to survive that night.

The emptiness that I've been living with—so utterly consuming—is what's left of a person when he dies and yet still breathes, facing each day with nothing at the end of it. When he exists, but cannot feel beyond his own misery. There's an endless weight on my chest that I will never be strong enough to lift off.

It's crushing my will.

And I finally accept that I'm done with this. I don't want to feel like this anymore.

So, I close my eyes and settle my head against the headrest. Just like I remember doing in the SUV that night.

And breathe in and out, slowly, heavily, over and over again.

Inhaling the fumes pumping in through the garden hose that hangs over the cracked window, the other end stuffed into the car's muffler.

The first genuine smile that I've felt in almost two years touches my lips.

A smile of relief, because peace is finally coming.

Chapter 14

May 2010

If I started to go bald, I'd just shave my head. I guess he's not exactly bald, but that hairline bought a one-way ticket and it's well on its way. I give him ten years before he's polishing his scalp.

"Hello? Trent?"

I blink several times, trying to focus on the doctor's words. "Sorry, what?"

He gives me a patient smile. "How are you feeling today?"

"Tired," I croak. A stomach pump for alcohol poisoning, serious oxygen therapy for carbon monoxide poisoning, and a slew of tests and psychological assessments has left me exhausted. Now I've got a mess of medication pumping through my veins. I'm not even sure how long I've been in this room, but I've been asleep most of that time.

Apparently, my dad came home from work minutes after I lost consciousness and, when he searched the house and couldn't find me, some gut-churning sixth sense told him to check the garage.

He couldn't get a pulse.

In my drunken stupor, I tried to kill myself. And I almost succeeded.

When I woke up in a hospital—again—with my mom holding my hand, tears in her eyes—again—and realized what I had done—again—I agreed to everything my dad started insisting upon, including an intense inpatient program. That's how I ended up in this sunny-colored, private Chicago cell.

It's not a cell, really. Though I haven't seen the rest of the facility yet, I'm guessing it's pretty nice.

"Your body has been through the ringer. You'll adjust. Ironically enough, I'm not a big fan of medicating, but I think, given the depth of your depression, you'll benefit from a small chemical reset."

Depression. That's what I keep hearing.

"So . . ." Dr. Stayner begins pacing, his arms over his chest, "you dropped out of college, quit the football team, broke up with your high school sweetheart, your parents are divorcing. And you spend excessive amounts of time in your mother's basement, isolating yourself with work."

"That about covers it," I mutter.

"It's been a long downward spiral for you." He pierces me with his stare. "Do you want to get better? Because that is a requirement for my inpatient program."

I'm betting this is the same opening spiel that he gives everyone. I don't mind, though, because the answer is simple. "Yes." I'm thinking clearly enough now—without scotch coursing through my veins, polluting my thoughts, amplifying my emotions—and I know that I don't have a choice. I've hit rock bottom and something has to change. It *has* to get better. I just don't think it's possible.

He slaps his hands together, like something's settled. His eyes twinkle with genuine excitement. "Good! We'll start therapy in the morning. Give you a swift kick in the ass, down the road to recovery. Until then, get some rest." He strolls briskly out of the room without another word, leaving me frowning at the door. My dad said that he's the best. I guess we'll see if the best is good enough.

■ ■ ■

My eyes follow the baseball as it sails up to nearly touch the spackled ceiling and then back down, landing in Dr. Stayner's hand with a soft thud.

Up and down.

Up and down.

"So, is ending your life something you gave a lot of thought to?"

I sigh, taking in his modest navy-blue carpeted office. Pretty much what you'd expect from a shrink: a desk, a few chairs, some framed certificates, and lots of books. "Honestly? No. I mean . . . I don't know how many nights I wished I'd gone to bed and simply not woken up, but I wasn't really planning on anything."

He nods like he understands. Does he, really? Or does that answer just fit the textbook definition of depression? "But that night . . ." he prods.

"That night . . ." I pick through my foggy recollection. Most of my thoughts veer toward the same thing nowadays anyway, so it's not hard to pinpoint. "I started thinking about how fucked up everything is, how many people I've hurt, and how I'll never escape this feeling. How maybe I wasn't meant to live. Then I thought it'd be a good idea to down half a bottle of scotch."

"A depressant cocktail to amplify your deep depression. That worked out well, didn't it . . ." The ball goes up and down. Oddly enough, it makes the entire conversation feel that much more casual. Like we're not talking about how I tried to kill myself. I wonder if that's a shrink technique. "How'd you end up in the car?"

An image of Kacey's face hits me. I'm not willing to bring her name into this conversation yet. Maybe because I don't want to admit that I carry her around in my phone. Maybe because I don't want to admit that I sat outside her house. I definitely don't want to admit what happened at that frat party. "I started wondering if being in a car will always be uncomfortable." That's one thing

Kacey and I seem to have in common, though her phobia is on an entirely different level.

He kicks his feet up onto his desk and leans back in his chair. "And what made you put the hose in the exhaust and start the car?"

"I don't want to feel like this anymore."

"What does it feel like?"

How can I possibly describe what's going on inside me? I don't think there's any way to do it justice. But I try. "Like I've been wandering along an old dirt road for two years with no end in sight. Not a soul around me." Again, Kacey's face flashes through my mind. The feel of her mouth against mine, her arms wrapped around mine, her body wanting mine. For her, it was just another drunken night, another moment's respite from her misery. For me, it was something deeper. On this endless, isolated journey, it was a momentary connection with the only other person to walk away from the accident. And it reminded me of what I'll never have again, because who the hell would want to be stuck on this lonely road with me?

When I glance up, Dr. Stayner's blue-gray eyes are dissecting me. Not in a "this idiot's going to pay for my kitchen reno" way; in a way that's full of compassion. I swallow against the forming lump. "So how are you gonna fix me?"

"Oh, I can't fix you, Trent. I'll take all the credit, mind you. It's a great boost to my ego. But *you* have to fix you."

Curiosity overcomes me. "You know my real name isn't Trent, right?"

"Yes, your parents filled me in on your history."

"So why are you calling me Trent? Do you agree that I should have changed my name?"

He shrugs. "Who do you want to be?"

"Not Cole Reynolds."

"Then I guess that makes you Trent Emerson, now doesn't it?" He tosses the ball a few more times. "I had a patient once. His name was Benny Flanagan, but he insisted that we call him Fidel Castro."

I can't stifle my snort. "What did you—"

"Fidel Castro." He chuckles. "Fiddy, for short. He had some very serious identity issues. But, eventually he remembered that he was Benny Flanagan."

"And what if I don't ever want to go back to being Cole Reynolds again?"

"What if you can't?" Dr. Stayner counters without missing a beat.

I frown. Is that a trick question?

He slaps the ball on his desk with a hard thud. "That's what this is all about. You can't go back. You can't change what happened. You can't resurrect the dead. You can only find ways to help yourself come to terms with it all. That's the only way you'll ever move on. What do you, Cole, Trent—whoever you want to be—need in order to move on? Because we can change where your future is heading. That's why you're here. We all want you to have a long and happy future."

"Okay . . ." What he's saying makes sense. To be honest, it's nothing I didn't already know. But when Dr. Stayner says it, I feel like he's giving me the permission that I can't give myself. "So, how am I going to fix myself?"

His feet slide unceremoniously off the desk. "Well, first and foremost, by remembering that you're human."

■ ■ ■

For a glorified mental hospital, this isn't so bad. It's not what I ever imagined a place like this to be. There are definitely no lunatics ranting about the end of the world or the army of voices in their heads. There are a lot of really nice people in private rooms and smiling staff to get you whatever you need; there's a gym that I've spent a good deal of time in; there's a small yard with oak trees and tiny purple flowers waking up after a long winter, and wooden benches you can sit on to enjoy the spring air.

Of course, I assume that not every place is like this. I'm sure my parents are paying for these niceties. I'll be working double-time to pay them back for this, whether they like it or not.

"Beautiful day."

I shield my eyes against the sun as a woman takes a seat, adjusting her long, brown ponytail over her shoulder. "Yeah, it's nice to feel the sun again." I grin to myself, realizing that I actually meant that.

"I'm Sheila." She holds a hand out, her eyes crinkling at the corners with her smile. I can't help but notice the pink slashes along the wrist that lies on her lap. "How long have you been here?"

"Almost two weeks. You?"

"Six weeks."

"That's a long time."

"That's a long time to deal with Dr. Stayner," she corrects, and we both share a chuckle. She pauses. "What are you in for?" She asks it so casually, proving to me that her time here has probably been well spent.

Two weeks ago, I couldn't care less about some stranger's plight or telling her about mine, because I'd been so swallowed up by my own turmoil that I didn't believe anything was going to get me out of it. But if my time in group therapy sessions has taught me anything, it's that talking about the accident and the aftermath with people who understand *does* actually help. And every single person in that session does understand. Or, at least, they can empathize. They didn't know Sasha and Derek, and they may not have been in a car accident, but some personal hardship has landed them here. And they don't judge me, because doing that quickly leads them to judging themselves.

In a room with these people, holding hands with all of our demons, I feel a sense of peace.

That's why I tell Sheila everything. I even tell her about Kacey, things I haven't admitted to Stayner. Not all the gritty details, but I think enough to make her see how much Kacey has come to mean to me.

How much I hope that she's all right.

That's my only regret, being in this place. There's no internet, no cell phones. No way for me to make sure that Kacey makes it home at night.

Sheila listens to the entire story, twirling the wedding band around her finger absently. And when it's her turn to talk, she takes a deep breath. And tells me about her eleven-month-old daughter, Claire, and how she turned her attention away from the happy, splashing baby sitting in a turtle pool with four inches of water for no more than ten seconds—she swears—while saying good-bye to guests.

And how Claire must have tried to get up but fell into the water.

And how Sheila found her, facedown and eerily still.

By the time she's done, my chest is heavy to the point of pain.

"I'm really sorry."

She smiles sadly, her gaze drifting out over the park-like setting. "So am I. I think I've said that word a thousand times. My husband hasn't forgiven me. He says he has, but I see it in his eyes. I don't blame him. I can't forgive myself either. I never will. But I think it'd help if I had forgiveness from him."

Silence settles over us.

And I ponder what it would be like to have Kacey's forgiveness. Would it lessen the burden of this weight just a little?

Would that be something too selfish to ask for?

■ ■ ■

"You made an incredibly stupid mistake," Dr. Stayner confirms matter-of-factly.

"Yeah, I know. Thanks. We've been over this already." Four weeks in group therapy sessions and private chats with the renowned doctor have taught me that I can say and do whatever I want without insulting or offending him. He seems to think the same applies to him with his patients.

"Imagine being Captain Edward J. Smith." My puzzled brow earns an eye roll. "The guy who plowed the unsinkable ship into an iceberg and sank it? Killing fifteen hundred people? Making world history?" His eyes are wide with disbelief. "You kids, these days . . . What do they teach you?"

I never know what I'm walking into when I step into Dr. Stayner's office.

"He ignored several warnings about the icebergs. Why? No one knows for sure. I'm guessing that he *assumed* that the builders were right and the ship was indestructible. Maybe he *assumed* that a ship that size would simply cut through an iceberg. Whatever the reason, he was responsible for that ship and that ship didn't change course. Because of his actions, or inactions, all those people died. Because of a *mistake*. Something that every human being makes."

Now I think I know where he's going with this. But maybe not. Stayner tends to go off on tangents now and again.

"You assumed that your friend was fine to drive because he'd never get behind the wheel drunk, just like you'd never get behind the wheel knowingly drunk, right?"

"Never," I answer without hesitation. I knew Sasha as well as I know myself.

"And he probably seemed fine to you at the time, because you yourself were drunk, and because you wanted to get home to study." He shrugs. "And because simple human nature operates under an 'it won't ever happen to me' mentality."

"Stop making excuses for me." We've been dancing this dance for a while now, where he tells me that I can't hold myself responsible and I tell him that I am responsible and no psychological mumbo jumbo will change that.

"I'm not making excuses for you. I'm just stating facts. Giving you reasons. The fact is, you didn't mean to hand keys over to your drunk friend. If you had known he was drunk, you probably would have waited and then driven yourself. Right?"

"Right, but—"

"And the fact is you didn't *intentionally* drink too much."

"Right, but that doesn't change that I did it."

"That's right. You did it. And you can't undo it. But your friend Sasha also asked you for the keys. And your friend Derek was perfectly capable of putting his seat belt on. So was Sasha. That was a choice they made—or didn't make—and they paid for it with their lives."

"And the Clearys? They didn't ask for this."

"No, they didn't," he agrees soberly. "They were just at the wrong place at the wrong time. Just think, if they hadn't stopped for pizza, if they didn't go to that game . . ."

A shudder runs through me. "I know." I've thought about it a lot. I'm sure Kacey has, too.

"But that's life, Trent. Whether we like it or not, we live and die by an endless stream of choices that affect each next step in our lives. Sometimes in ways we never dared think of or hoped for. Sometimes in ways we can't make sense of for a long time.

I'm trying to help you make sense of what happened because the sooner you do that, the sooner you can move on. You made a *mistake*, Trent. A mistake of drinking too much and believing that your friend was fine to drive. Sasha made the mistake of thinking he was fine to drive. Sasha and Derek made the mistake of not wearing their seat belts. And all those mistakes turned into a tragic accident that claimed six people's lives."

He pauses, as if to let his words sink into my head. "I told my sons about this very case last night over dinner. They're still too young to drive, but I like to scare the snot out of them with real-life scenarios every once in a while."

"Isn't that unethical?"

He waves my doubtful tone away with his free hand. "The accident is public knowledge."

"What about everything else?" I wouldn't be surprised if Dr. Stayner has provided a play-by-play review of our conversation to his kids over a plate of fried chicken. In the time that I've been here, I've quickly learned that the patient, pragmatic doctor is also a loud and insistent man, willing to roll up his sleeves and climb into the trenches with his patients. He pushes boundaries and he doesn't mince words. Sometimes that causes problems. Last week, I saw him tearing out of this very office and toward the orderlies, a distraught patient hot on his heels, shrieking at him. They had to sedate her. Two days ago, he had a three-hundred-pound man named Terrence sobbing uncontrollably.

He says both of those cases were major breakthroughs.

I'll reserve my judgment on that for now.

"I didn't tell them the rest. Would you like me to? Or, better yet . . ." He holds up the large navel orange sitting on his desk, which has held my attention for some reason, and then tosses it to me. "Would *you* like to? Because I can guarantee you that your story matters. You can't save your friends or the people in the other car. That's in the past. But you can save lives now. In the future. When I talk about making amends, that's the kind of thing I'm talking about."

"So you finally agree that this was my fault," I mutter wryly.

He throws his hands up in frustration. "I agree that you think it's your fault. I can't change that. You need to change that. Or accept it and move on. And the only way you're going to do that is by easing your guilt. Feeling like you can earn some level of forgiveness. And the only way to do that is by making the amends that you feel you need to make. So, how about we draw a line in the sand and move on. Agree?"

I nod.

He drags a stubby finger across his desk. "Line drawn. Now we just need to figure out what your amends look like."

Chapter 15

June 2010

"We haven't spent much time talking about the girl who survived. What was her name?"

"Kacey Cleary."

"Right. And how often do you think about this Kacey girl?"

I shrug, twisting a shoelace between my fingers. "I don't know. Sometimes it's a lot. Sometimes not so much." Such an ambiguous answer. Such a lie. I wonder if Stayner sees it. He probably does. The shrewd doc never seems to miss anything.

If he does, he lets it go for now. "That's normal. You feel like you've wronged her."

"I *have* wronged her."

He doesn't argue with me anymore about that. "Your father told me that you went to visit her once in the hospital?"

"Yeah. But I didn't have the guts to actually see her."

"Have you thought about trying to see her again?"

I'm guessing lying won't do me any good here. "Yeah." I pause. "Are you going to tell me I shouldn't?" He's going to tell me that I shouldn't. I really fucking hope he doesn't, because I damn well already know that I will.

He shrugs. "From what your father told me, it sounds like she's had a rough go of things. She might not be so receptive to seeing you. And if you're not completely at peace with where you're at, I'm afraid it could set you back down a dark path that you don't want to be on. You need to focus on yourself right now."

I sigh. He's probably right.

"You feel you need some form of closure from her?"

Another nod. "Or something." I'm afraid to say more.

Pulling a pad of lined paper and a pen out from a drawer, he tosses them on the desk in front of me. "Write it out. Everything you want to say to her. I don't need to see it. But get it all out, and then leave it at that. In time, she may seek you out. You can give it to her then, if you want. Or you can say it out loud." He pauses. "Just be prepared that she may not ever want to meet you and she deserves to make that call. Wouldn't you agree?"

I sigh. It's not exactly what I want to hear.

■ ■ ■

I lie in the twin bed in my sunny little room, pondering everything that Stayner has said. That's one thing he gets me doing. Thinking. It's like the guy has a wizard's wand.

I think about Kacey Cleary as I always do—wondering how she's doing right now, hoping that she's not getting herself into trouble. How much farther can she spiral? I guess she could hit rock bottom, like I did. Maybe she has already. What if I'm released from here to find out the worst? All of my time with Dr. Stayner will have been worthless; I'm sure of it. For so many reasons, both selfish and not.

Because I want her to be free of this.

And because while I can make as many amends as I want, I don't think I'll ever truly move on until she does.

Until that sparkle in her eye comes back, that smile shines bright again.

The pad of paper lies across my chest; where it has stayed for hours, rows upon rows of scratched-out sentences. Because there are just no words.

Only a wish.

■ ■ ■

Stayner's handshake is as firm as I would expect from a man of his integrity and strength.

"You ready to be released into the wild again?" he asks, a proud smile on full display. He *should* be proud. He's given me strength and focus.

A purpose.

I chuckle. "Yeah, I guess." It feels weird, leaving these walls five weeks later, considering the state I entered them in. But I think I'm ready.

Stayner frowns. "What's going on in your head, Trent? You're hung up on something, aren't you?"

Damn guy. I can't say no or he'll probably shred the release papers. Not that I can't leave of my own accord—this isn't prison. But I promised my parents that I'd see it through and I have every intention of doing that. So I admit vaguely, "I'm nervous. About everything. About seeing people again. About seeing my parents after what I put them through."

He slaps my shoulder, like I'd imagine a father would do to his son. "Do you know how happy they are today, waiting out there in the parking lot? Knowing that they're getting their son back?"

I bite my tongue against the urge to argue that I'm not the same person anymore. "Yes, but they're still divorcing. They've still lost their entire retirement fund. I can't change that."

He nods solemnly. "You're right. You can't. That's a challenge that the two of them—and their relationship—must face. But any good parents will give all the money in the world to keep their child alive and well. I've met your parents. They're good people, Trent. So, you just focus on you. You have a solid recovery plan in place, people who love you, and, most important, you have amends to make."

I nod. He's right about that.

Pushing through the doors of the clinic, I see my dad's SUV parked out front. He and my mom slide out of their seats, hopeful smiles on their faces.

All it takes is a returning smile and my mom's eyes water.

Holding up my finger—asking them for a minute—I slip my phone out of my pocket and hit number three on my speed dial.

"Hello?" It's as hollow as ever, but it's her voice.

I hit the "end" button and feel relief wash over me. Kacey's still here. She's still hanging on. That's all I can hope for right now. I can feel the folded note in my back pocket, the one that maybe I'll be able to give her one day. Maybe. But Stayner's right; it's not fair that I seek her out for my own healing.

So I'll stay away from her.

For now.

Chapter 16

September 2010

Her hands rub the transfer onto my back with slow, smooth swipes. "What language is this?"

"Latin."

"Huh . . . Sit up straight. Is this good?"

I follow her instructions and use the mirror in front to see the reflection in the one she's holding up to my shirtless back. The heavy black lettering stretches from blade to blade. "Perfect."

"Okay, Trent. Ready for your first tattoo?" I see the sparkle in her gaze, the sensual curve of her smile, as she holds the tattoo gun in one hand. I wonder if she'd still be giving me those fuck-me eyes if she knew I was in an inpatient rehab for attempted suicide only a few months ago.

Not that it matters. My attention is on one girl now and I won't let it get divided.

"I'm ready. Let's do this."

■ ■ ■

"Hello?" Impatience fills her voice.

And I immediately break out in a sweat. "Is James there?"

"James? No. There is no James at this number. Learn how to dial!" Full irritation now. But she's sober. I've called on three different Saturday nights and she's been coherent each time. That says something. Maybe her spiral has stopped. Maybe she's getting better.

I need to know.

She hangs up on me, as she has the last two times I phoned and asked for James.

The next call I make is to Rich. "Hey! Cole! How's it going?"

I grit my teeth but say nothing. Rich knows me as Cole. That's never going to change and I can't expect him to just start calling me by something different. Stayner helped me rationalize that. Holding on to some ties to my past, as much as I'm not really that guy anymore, will keep me grounded. "I'm good."

"I tried calling a couple times." Did he hear what happened? I figure my mom might have told Derek's mom. They still talk, occasionally.

"Sorry, man. I've been busy." That's not a lie. When Stayner's clinic doors closed behind me, I stepped out, running. Within days I had located and attended my first PTSD support group. I go to it weekly. Through that, I've made connections with a local-area high school and two elementary schools. I'm in talks to give presentations to some of the classes about the dangers of drinking and driving. I'll probably shit my pants, but it's something I need to do. Stayner was one hundred percent on the mark. I can't change what happened, but I have a story to tell, one that could make an impact on other people's lives. What better way to start making my amends?

"You've gotta come down again soon."

"Maybe in a few months?" It's taken me everything not to jump in my car and head straight for a certain brick house just outside of Grand Rapids. But it's too risky. I don't know what seeing me would do to Kacey. Or what it might do to me.

"I'm still in the apartment. Decided to do my PhD."

I chuckle. "Derek always said you didn't want to join the real world." It feels good, being able to share a laugh about my friend again, without my insides burning. "Listen, I have a favor to ask of you."

"Shoot. Whatever I can do to help."

I hesitate. This idea of mine may be crazy—in fact, I know it is. I can't recall exactly when I came up with it. Probably around the same time that I realized keeping tabs on her would be impossible from six hours away. "Do you still have that hacker friend of yours?"

"Uh . . . yeah. Why?"

"What does it cost to get into someone's email account?"

Chapter 17

June 2011

"I'm glad I caught you."

"Hey, Mom."

"How's condo hunting? Did you check out that neighborhood I was telling you about?"

I can hear the hopefulness in her voice. That neighborhood is a seven-minute drive from her house. When I first told her that I felt it was time to invest in a place of my own, she struggled to hide the panic. As well as I'm doing—genuinely; it's not an act this time around—she still rushes to get home for dinner every night. She still calls me every afternoon if I haven't called or texted her yet; I wake up to a door creak almost every night, sensing her hovering over my bed, listening to me breathe.

She never used to be like this. Stayner warned me to expect it. From both her and my dad. I'd get a lot of questions and concerned looks and general overprotectiveness for a long time. They almost lost me, after all. Twice.

"Uh . . . yeah. We'll see, Mom. Listen, I may stay over at a friend's house tonight."

"Oh? Which friend?"

"*Mom.*"

She sighs. "Right. Sorry. Okay, just text me so I don't worry. I miss you."

Between the courses I'm taking at a local college and all the work I'm doing—both for my mom and some freelance stuff for small businesses who can't afford to run print ads but might need a logo or marketing pamphlet design—plus the weekly group sessions and M.A.D.D. stuff I'm involved in, and a healthy gym schedule, I'm barely home.

"I will. Love you." The truth is, I'm getting to the point where I need more space, more freedom to come and go without explanation.

Without having to lie.

Like today, when I strolled out the door at six a.m., I had to tell her I was heading to the gym. I was lucky she didn't ask why I had bothered showering. And now, here I am, almost six hours away in this Caledonia Starbucks, having lied to her. I've been here since noon, making myself comfortable in a back corner, with a steady stream of caffeine to keep me going, my laptop open in front of me.

Kacey Cleary's private email in-box staring at me.

I should feel guilty about invading her privacy—a small part of me does—but I'm not doing it to hurt her. And, I have my limits. When Rich's hacker connection offered to hack into the webcam that's connected to her family's home computer for an extra grand, I told him I'd hunt him down and beat the shit out of him if he did that.

What it's given me is a small glimpse into Kacey Cleary. A small window. Not one that I could actually fit through, but at least now I know just a tiny bit about Kacey Cleary. Information that I jot down in a little notebook. Things I can't possibly forget.

Like, that Kacey has no friends.

Well, maybe that's not fair for me to say, but in the eight months since I've been keying the password "douchebags" into her Hotmail account, I haven't seen a single email from a friend. Maybe they just don't email each other.

To be honest, there isn't much in her in-box for me to work

with. Mostly spam, including all the counseling newsletters and support group information blasts I signed her up for. That she hasn't bothered to even delete, let alone open.

I know that she finished her senior year of high school, even if it was a year late. Based on a few old emails from her counselor, requesting meetings to discuss her grades and what options she has for improving on them, she didn't do it with flying colors. I have to commend her for not quitting, though. Not like I did.

I also know that she started working at Starbucks last summer. It sounds like she's here almost every day now, picking up extra shifts every time this manager guy, Jake, emails her. They were only occasional emails at first, with just her schedule. But over the months, he's begun tagging cheesy and borderline inappropriate jokes onto each request. It's obvious to anyone that he's flirting with her. At least, *I* see it.

That's why I finally broke the rule I made on the day I was released and drove out here today. Because when I read this last message, I decided that I needed to know once and for all.

To: Kacey Cleary
From: Jake Rogers, Starbucks Management
Date: June 11, 2011
Re: 3–11 shift this Sunday
Hey, Red – Can you work this Sunday? Joanne has a family thing.
I'll be there ☺

To: Jake Rogers, Starbucks Management
From: Kacey Cleary
Date: June 11, 2011
Re: 3–11 shift this Sunday
I'll take the shift. Despite you being there.

No smiley face. No LOL. No indication that she's kidding. It feels like a blow-off.

That night, I lay in bed, wondering if there was something going on between her and this Jake guy. What if he's taking advantage of her? What if they're together?

I couldn't fall asleep for hours. So I decided that I had to risk it.

It could be a boneheaded move. She may know what I look like. Not that she'd remember me from the frat party. I know I look different from my college days—my hair now shaggy, my face perpetually covered in scruff. I'm leaner than I was back then, but hard.

Just in case, I grabbed a baseball cap and wore a loose jacket, trying not to attract too much attention from my corner, in front of an obscure mirror on the wall that shows the entire counter space. From here, I can hear their conversation perfectly.

I just need to see them together for two minutes and I'll know if she's got a thing for the douche canoe I've been eyeing for the better part of two hours—a cross between Carrot Top and the Fonz.

If she does?

My chest floods with disappointment at the thought.

And suddenly Kacey's just there, standing behind the counter in a black employee golf shirt. She must have come in through a back door because there's no way I would have missed her. I suck in a breath. It feels like a lifetime has passed between the last time I saw her face and now, more than a year ago. Where I was mentally, then and now.

But, more importantly, where is *she*? I don't know what else she's been doing, but it can't be filling her nostrils with cocaine and her stomach with alcohol anymore. As fit as she looked before, she's all sinewy now, her arms corded, her movements reminding me of a leopard—sleek and graceful and dangerous. Her face hasn't changed, in that it's still hard and unyielding, the smiles fake and fleeting, and never reaching her eyes. Those watery blue eyes that haven't found their sparkle again.

Will they ever? Why isn't she getting help? Why is no one making her get help! It's been over three years.

Her face also *has* changed, though. She was a pretty girl before.

Now, at nineteen, she's a stunning woman.

So much so that I struggle to peel my eyes from her reflection as she begins serving customers and pouring coffees, always polite but never warm. It's almost like she's mentally not here. That she's put herself on autopilot, not really noticing her surroundings beyond her purpose for being here.

Kind of like I was for so long.

Until she steps out from behind the counter, that is, and begins weaving around tables, collecting dishes and trash left behind, those strong, lean legs in black, fitted shorts stirring the blood in my body.

And panic.

I duck my head as she passes around my back.

"Done with those?" She swoops in and collects my dishes without my answer, my nostrils filling with the scent of soap and shampoo. I'm guessing she just came from the gym.

"Sure, thanks," I mutter to her back as she walks away. She doesn't seem interested in making eye contact. Or any contact. With anyone. It's for the best, at this point, though just once I'd like to lock eyes with her, feel them on me. And know what she knows.

Know if she realizes this connection we share, being the only two people to walk away from that night, to get stuck in the vortex of its aftermath, unable to move on. Would she hate me for it?

Or would it help her to know that she's not alone? Not anymore. Not with me here.

Those are the thoughts I can't shake. But the great news is that she ignores Jake for the most part, throwing him only enough of a bone to keep him happy. A tiny, emotionless smile, a flat giggle. Smart on her part, with him being her manager and all. He seems to drink the attention up like a lapdog.

And she continues *existing*.

I can tell she hasn't gotten any better. She may not be tumbling anymore. Maybe she did hit rock bottom, like I did. But I don't think she's started her climb back up yet.

What if I could help her take the first steps? Someone has to.

I really should leave.

In another twenty minutes.

■ ■ ■

September 2011

We stopped attending mass when I was around twelve. There was no big political reason behind it; we just stopped going. I don't think I've been in a church—outside of Sasha's funeral—in the eleven years since. Yet the second I step inside, I'm hit with that familiar smell that I recognize immediately. A strange combination of wood and must and incense.

It seems almost fitting that I've broken my rule to stay away a second time to come to church, seeking answers. Specifically, why haven't Kacey's aunt and uncle gotten her help?

It took me four trips to Caledonia and risky stakeout sessions to find the parish that her aunt, Darla, attends for Sunday morning services as well as on Mondays for prayer. It's a small, old church with brown brick and a tall, narrow steeple.

Darla's seated in the fourth pew from the front right side, her short, curly black hair sprayed in place, her forehead resting against clasped hands as she prays. I slowly pick my steps down the aisle, easing into the pew behind her and a good ten feet over. Given that it's Monday and we're alone in here, I'm fully aware that this is a weird move on my part. But I'm hoping I'm right about her.

Turns out, I am.

"So nice to see a young man in church, praying," she whispers with a smile my way.

I return the smile. "I'll admit, it's been a while."

"Are you from around here?"

"Just visiting some friends." I hate lying, what with Jesus hanging on a cross directly in front of me.

She nods as if in agreement. "I know almost every parishioner here. I didn't think I'd seen you around."

With that, she turns back to her prayers, and I silently try to plan out how I'm going to get information from her. After half an hour, I realize that the woman is either a marathon worshipper or she has a lot to worry about. Either way, my ass is getting sore against the hard wood and I've given up on this brilliant plan of mine. The pew creaks loudly, echoing through the lofty space, as I stand and walk toward the aisle.

"Do keep your faith up. It's so difficult to get young people in here and they're the ones who need it most, what with all the drugs and sex and violence in society today."

So . . . Aunt Darla's not a partier. Does she have any clue what her niece has been doing? "You're right," I agree. "Do your kids come with you?"

"Oh, I don't have children. But my nieces live with me and one of them has started coming to confession on Friday afternoons, after school. Now, if I could just get my other one here . . ."

"Not interested in religion?" *Come on, Darla. Give me more.*

Darla's tight smile tells me she's biting her tongue. "Kacey's not interested in much of anything," she mutters, and then adds for my benefit, "She lost her parents in a tragic car accident."

I frown appropriately. "It must be hard to deal with, for her."

"Well, Livie lost her parents too and she didn't become a heathen," she argues. "Then again, I suppose Livie wasn't the one stuck in the car, waiting to be pulled out."

A genuine frown pulls my brow together.

She sees my bewilderment. "It took those firefighters hours to cut into the car. How she remained conscious that entire time is beyond me."

Thankfully I'm still in the row because my knees give out and I half-sit, half-fall into the pew. I can feel the muscles in my face fighting to control my expression, trying to hide the horror from it. Kacey sat in a car with her dead parents. Just the idea of seeing Sasha or Derek lying on the pavement is enough to drain the blood from my face.

"It's divine intervention, is what I keep saying to her," Aunt Darla keeps going. "How can no one believe there's a God after that? The girl should have died, to be honest. I tell her that and she just gets angry. Angrier . . ." She harrumphs. "She's never anything *but* angry nowadays. She was always the boisterous one of the two, getting into mischief and all. But it was good-natured, before. She loved life. Now . . ."

I blow out a mouthful of air. "Sounds like she needs some help."

"I've tried, but she refuses. She still has nightmares every night. Her screams are . . ." She shudders. "I haven't had a good night's sleep in more than two years, since she moved in with us."

Yeah, poor you. "Is she seeing a therapist or going to support groups or . . . anything?"

One shake confirms my fears. Kacey is exactly like I was. "She's beyond help. I had the church counselor and the priest visit our house, but Kacey would have none of that. I even bought her her own Bible and left it on her nightstand. The spine hasn't been cracked once." She clucks her tongue. "If only my sister raised them with God in their lives, Kacey would be fine now. I truly believe that."

I'm not so sure about that. One of Dr. Stayner's patients in the program was an ex-nun named Margaret, whose two-year-old niece snuck out the front door and got hit by a car while Margaret was babysitting. She walked away from her church and her beliefs after that. Even the most God-fearing person's faith can be displaced when tragedy strikes. Maybe for only a short time; maybe forever.

"Well, it was nice talking to you." That's partly true. Now I know exactly how Kacey's doing according to her aunt, who sounds pretty damn unsympathetic. I'm guessing she doesn't mean to be. She just doesn't know what to do except pray.

I can't help but wonder, if Kacey had a Dr. Stayner in her life, would she be completely different?

Aunt Darla smiles warmly. "I hope to see you here again, soon. There's a new, young priest here now. Just started this week."

"Maybe I'll be back."

Maybe Friday.

■ ■ ■

What if Livie knows what I look like?

She probably does. Just because her sister now lives in a world where nothing—and nobody—matters, her younger sister seems stable. And probably curious.

I've reminded myself of that on the entire drive here. My second time making this trip this week. And yet I couldn't stop myself from coming.

I take a seat in a dark corner at the back of the church, hidden from most of the pews and the confessional booths. I don't know what the hell I think I'm going to accomplish, coming here, besides watching from the shadows. When I spot her long, shiny black hair, my stomach begins to churn.

I'm an idiot.

Her aunt is with her, encouraging her toward the confessional box with a prodding hand against her back and a broad smile. She reminds me a lot of Mrs. Wilcox, who lived down the street from us, growing up. That woman could recite every last line of the Bible and as a result, believed she could do and say no wrong.

The new, young priest excuses himself from his confessional booth with an apology just as Livie steps inside. By the way he's awkwardly jogging, I assume he needs the can. He reemerges a few minutes later, a bounce in his step. Only, then a woman scurries out from a side door, calling urgently after him.

"Can it wait?" I hear him ask.

Her head shakes in answer. "It'll only take five minutes. Ten minutes, at most."

With a frazzled glance at the little booth, he disappears through the door.

I only wanted to catch a glimpse of Livie. But what if I could get more than that? What if I . . .

Darla's head hangs low as she prays.

It's now or never.

If I wasn't going to hell before, I'm definitely going now. But I don't let that deter me from sliding into the empty booth, keeping the door cracked ever so slightly, a watchful eye on the room where the priest disappeared.

Now what the hell do I do? For as long as it's been since I've gone to mass, it's been at least that long since I've been to confession. Does the priest talk first? The confessor? *Shit!*

Thankfully, Livie takes care of that. "Bless me, Father, for I have sinned. It has been one week since my last confession." Her voice is hovering in that in-between stage, where she no longer sounds like a little girl but she's not really a woman yet.

"Continue." It's all I can think of, and then I purse my lips, waiting for her to scream, "Fraud!" That, or this door is about to be thrown open and I'm gonna have to make a run for it.

"Okay, so I'm lying to you already. I'm so sorry. I'm not here for me. I know you're not supposed to go to confession for another person, but Father Murray and I had an agreement." Her words tumble out of her mouth. "I'm here for my sister. She needs all the help that she can get."

My breath hitches. "Continue."

She heaves a sigh. "Thank you, Father. So, Kacey is her name. And I'm Livie. Anyway, last weekend she threatened to set fire to the Bible that my aunt keeps leaving on her nightstand."

I struggle to stifle my chuckle. It's not funny, really, and yet knowing that Kacey might still have some spunk buried deep inside gives me hope.

Livie doesn't seem to notice. "And she's saying all kinds of things about our uncle. Bad things."

"What kind of bad things?"

"That he's . . ." She drops her voice. "That he is starting to look at me *that* way."

"What way?" I snap, and then check my tone. "I mean, do you see that?"

"No! He's always been nice to me. Granted, he's usually drunk."

Huh. So saintly Aunt Darla doesn't have such a saintly husband.

"And your sister? Is she drinking? Or hurting herself in any other way?" I know that's a risky question to ask, but I need to know.

"No, not for over a year now."

Really? "What made her stop?"

"Me. I think. I mean, I tried not to let it all get to me. Be strong for her, you know? But one night, I was sitting up with her, like usual—"

"You sit up with her?"

"Well, yeah. I used to. I *had* to. And on this one night she started throwing up in her sleep and then choking on it. If I hadn't been there . . ."

Livie would have lost her sister.

I would have lost Kacey.

I shake my head, amazed at how strong and smart this little girl seems to be. "And now?"

"Now all she cares about is kickboxing."

That explains that rock-hard body of hers. A body I shouldn't be having thoughts about right now, as I pretend to be a priest and pump her little sister for information.

I'm *so* going straight to hell.

Livie's words cut into my private, dirty thoughts. "That, and making enough money to move out."

All thoughts of Kacey's body vanish. "Where does your sister want to move?"

"Oh, who knows? It's not likely to happen. I just started high school and my uncle gambled our inheritance away, so it's not like we can support ourselves."

Strike two for Uncle Raymond.

I hesitate before I ask, "What happened to your parents? . . . My child." *Man*, that sounded awkward.

Her voice drops, sadness filling it. "They died in a car accident, a little over three years ago now. A bunch of college guys, coming home from a party. Driving drunk."

"I'm sorry to hear that." I swallow, afraid to ask the question but knowing I'll probably never get another chance like this. "Do you or your sister ever think about talking to them?"

"Well, we can't. They died. Two of them did, anyway. One lived. I don't know where he is now."

"Perhaps it would give your sister some closure to see him. Talk to him?"

"Kacey?" Livie snorts. "No, I don't think that'd help her. Kacey wants nothing to do with anything that reminds her of the accident. I don't think she cares whether she lives or dies, to be honest."

I could sit here all day with Livie, but I'm starting to get anxious, my eyes darting furtively through the crack. Any minute now, that priest is going to appear. I can't be here when he does. "It sounds like you are a very good sister. She's very lucky to have you."

There's a long pause and then I hear the low whisper. "I just want her to get better."

So do I. "Say ten Hail Marys for your sister." And I will too, though I know she needs so much more than that.

"Thank you, Father."

"No. Thank *you*, Livie."

Chapter 18

January 2012

From what I can see, O'Malley's isn't a gym for the average Joe. That's what the website says, anyway. This place focuses on high-endurance sports like boxing and MMA fighting. And the kickboxing classes that Kacey takes. Led by this jackass, I surmise, looking at the picture of a sweaty, rippled guy in nothing but shorts and covered in tattoos—I'm assuming it's him—nailing his opponent in the face with his elbow.

> To: Kacey Cleary
> From: Jeff T.
> Re: Strike combo from my match last week
> Stay late and I'll teach you how to do this. Just you and me.

Just you and me. "Fucking asshole," I mutter. What kind of coach sends pictures of himself to his students? *A* student. A beautiful red-haired girl named Kacey, with a chip on her shoulder. I've been good, staying away from Kacey and her family since the confessional hijack. Up until I read this email. It wasn't hard to figure out where she goes. It's the only gym of this kind in town.

The smell of sweat and cleaner hits my nostrils the second I step in.

"Doors close in fifteen," the young punk behind the desk hollers at me, flexing his biceps—proudly on display in a wife-beater—as he sizes me up. I've got a sweatshirt on and the hoodie pulled over my head. Totally acceptable against the frigid blast of a winter storm outside right now.

I stifle my smirk. I'm twice the size of him. "Just wanted to check the place out, actually. Do you think you could give me a quick tour?"

He shrugs and then slides out of his chair, fingering the heavy gold chain around his neck as he comes around the counter, amplifying a swagger that he probably practices on a daily basis in front of his mirror. His pants hang halfway down his thighs, held up by a belt.

Sash and I used to make so much fun of those idiots.

"Where you from?"

"Detroit. What are the hours here?"

He starts rambling off information as he walks me through the main room, with the fighting ring and the punching bags. I'm beginning to think she's not here, until we pass by a set of doors.

He skirts past it. "There's a class going on in there right—"

"Great." I push through the door and stick my head in. Three sets of guys square off against each other, practicing combat moves. And, in the corner, a red-haired girl punches the shit out of a sandbag.

Jesus.

I hear the desk clerk talking behind me but I ignore him, all my focus on Kacey as she hammers that bag over and over again like an unstoppable machine, sweat soaking through the pair of tight shorts and the T-shirt she's wearing, her muscles straining. And then she seems to decide her T-shirt is in her way because she stops just long enough to tear if off her body and whip it at the ground, leaving her in only those shorts and a cropped sports bra.

Giving seven sets of eyes one helluva body to look at. And they do.

The guy from the picture is holding the kick bag, a wide grin on his face as he watches her continue. Like he's proud of her. Like he doesn't feel all the rage and hurt and pain that I can feel radiating from her all the way over here.

"Great job, Kacey!" He lets go of the bag, forcing her to stop, her chest heaving in and out as she attempts to catch her breath.

"Yo," the idiot clerk behind me calls, loud enough to attract attention.

I duck out just as Kacey turns my way. *That was close.* "Thanks. I'll be back later this week to sign all the papers," I lie, taking long, fast strides out of the gym until I'm back in the safety of my car, my heart racing.

And I wait. As snow pelts my car from all angles, I wait for almost an hour, long after all the gym rats have left and the lights are off, until my gas gauge is hovering over empty and I'm one of only two cars in the parking lot.

My agitation growing with each breath.

When the door finally cracks open, it's to let Kacey and her "coach" out, both their heads hidden within hoods and bowed against the snow. He throws an arm over her shoulder and my gut clenches. She shrugs it off immediately.

I crack my window slightly to listen, letting a blast of cold air into my otherwise toasty car.

"Why not?"

"Because I'm not interested. And if you don't stop hitting on me, I'm going to drop your stupid class."

With a light chuckle, he answers, "No you're not. You love my class."

"No, I *like* your class. But I don't need it anymore. I could save the money. In fact, consider this my notice."

The smile stretches across my mouth before I can help it. She's not into him. That makes me happier than it should.

"Whoa! Take it easy!" He lifts his hands in surrender and she begins marching toward the black pickup parked beside me. She moves past it, though.

"Where are you going?" Jeff calls out after her.

"Home."

His head drops back, like he's exasperated with her. I don't doubt Kacey tests people's patience on a regular basis. "Don't be stupid. Come on, let me give you a ride home."

"Don't need it."

Fuck. Is she nuts? We're in the middle of nowhere, at night, in a blizzard, and her house is at least two miles away.

"You're going to freeze, Kacey!"

"No, I'm not. I'm just not going with you." Suddenly she's turning. And walking toward my passenger-side door. And throwing my door open.

Holy shit.

I sink back into my hood as casually as possible, thanking God that I still have it on.

Willing myself not to turn and give her a good look at my face. Even in the dark, it's too risky.

The thing is, she doesn't even turn to look at me. It's like she doesn't even care whose car she climbed into. "Do you mind dropping me off at the corner of Main and Church?"

"Um. Sure," I mumble, keeping my voice low, in case by some crazy chance she may recognize it. Pathetic disguise. I pull out of the parking lot, my car slipping and sliding as we creep along the dead streets in silence. Her fingertips—the ones I held for almost an hour that night so long ago—tap against a thigh. I'm betting any edge she feels right now has nothing to do with being in a car with a complete stranger, but with being in a car, period.

I wonder if she can tell I'm ready to shit my pants. How the hell do I keep getting myself into these situations with her? Oh yeah . . . because I'm basically stalking her.

"Just up at this corner on the right is fine."

I know that the second I stop, she's jumping out. So I don't wait to ask, "Do you normally get into the car with complete strangers?"

She doesn't miss a beat. "Do you normally drive complete strangers around when they get into your car?"

She has a point, I guess. Still . . . "I could be a murderer."

"Well then make it quick, or pull over because I need to be up early for work tomorrow." Completely deadpan, no hint of humor. No hint of fear.

Kacey's clearly not afraid of anything anymore, and that's a scary place to be. Every person needs a healthy dose of fear, something that gets their blood rushing. Something they can't bear to lose.

My brakes squeak as I stop. And, just as I expected, Kacey is gone with barely a "thanks" trailing behind her, a solitary figure disappearing into a blur of snow and darkness.

■ ■ ■

It takes twenty minutes under the shower nozzle at the roadside motel to warm the chill from my bones after tonight. I still can't seem to shake the odd buzz coursing through my body. The one that Kacey left behind. I can't quite explain it. She's so dark, so harsh, so wounded. Her prickly exterior would keep most everyone away.

And yet all I want to do is get closer.

Break through that wall she has erected to feel the warmth that I just know used to be there. That's hidden by that sharp tongue and powerful body.

That body . . .

Blood begins rushing downward as an image of her in those tight shorts hits me, with one of those asses that seems unreal, as hard and round as it is. That would feel incredible in my hands. As would the rest of her.

Shit.

There's no point lying to myself; the raging hard-on now gripped firmly in my palm is impossible to ignore.

I'm seriously attracted to Kacey.

"Fuck." My forehead falls to the tile. It was one thing when I was just looking out for her. Though who the hell am I kidding? How long ago did she hook me? The visit to Starbucks, this trip tonight . . . When did this become about more than watching out for her, about making amends?

I need to get some space. No more visits. No more close calls. But what if . . .

What if she could learn to love again? And what if *I'm* the one who can remind her what that feels like?

Chapter 19

April 26, 2012

How fitting, that the first warm day of spring is today of all days. It's perfect, really, since I've been sitting on this bench for six hours.

Waiting.

I was here to greet the groundskeeper this morning at eight o'clock, when he eased the cemetery gates open. With flowers in one hand and directions to the tombstones in the other, I made my way through the small Catholic cemetery. It was extremely easy to find where the Clearys were laid to rest. The information was in that thin yellow folder that my dad now keeps at the back of his home-office filing cabinet, along with a number and a receipt for a local florist that will deliver straight to gravesites. My parents, as thoughtful as they are, sent flowers on the first and second and third anniversaries of the accident. Based on the florist truck that's pulling up near the graveyard now, and the bouquet of flowers that the deliveryman has in one hand, I'd bet money that they plan on doing this every year until they die.

I wonder if Kacey knows who they're from.

If she even comes.

I can't believe that she won't. Then again, I'm not in Rochester to stop by Sasha's graveyard today.

But they're her parents.

I haven't seen Kacey since that night back in January, keeping myself busy at my new condo and with work. There isn't a day that hasn't gone by, though, that I don't think about her, or check in on her email.

Twice I've called her, just to hear her voice.

But I had to come today. You can learn a lot about a person from poignant moments like an anniversary at the grave of someone that person loved. Things you definitely can't learn through reading email or spying in coffee shops.

And so I sit on this bench, watching from behind my thick aviator sunglasses as people filter through the cemetery to leave flowers and words of longing to their loved ones. The sun plays hide-and-seek behind billowing clouds, and I absorb the heat from its rays in a way that I didn't allow myself to for so long.

And I wait for her.

If I thought for a second that she'd recognize me, I wouldn't be here. But, for all the times she's seen me, she's never really looked at me. She's never so much as made eye contact.

Finally, the navy-blue Camry—the one I recognize as Aunt Darla's—pulls up. Sliding off the bench, I take six quick steps to kneel before a random stone, offering my apologies to Jorge Mastracci for using his resting place as a cover.

The car is barely in park when Kacey jumps out of the backseat. I can't really see her face. The top half is hidden behind giant dark sunglasses. The bottom half looks rigid, as usual.

She hangs back like a statue as her sister and aunt approach the twin tombstones, Livie hugging a large wreath of purple flowers, her aunt with a rosary dangling from her fingers, both wearing solemn expressions. Even from this distance, I can see Kacey's throat bob up and down as she swallows repeatedly. As she fights against the emotions. I know that she's a fighter. She's strong. But, after four years, she needs to find a way to let go.

How much longer can she go on like this?

"Are you kidding me?" Suddenly Kacey's diving toward the

graves. Only when she stands up with a bouquet of flowers and tosses them to the side, her mouth pressed in a thin line of anger, do I know.

"Kacey!" her aunt cries out, her mouth hanging open. Livie doesn't say a word, simply scooping the flowers up and adjusting some of the bent petals. She makes a move to place them back.

"Don't you dare, Livie." The iciness in Kacey's tone as she warns her sister off sends chills down my spine.

"It's a nice gesture," Livie argues in a soft, even tone. A tone much too old for a fifteen-year-old to be using.

Snatching the bouquet from her sister's hand, Kacey marches off.

I bow my head, my heart speeding up with each angry step as she cuts through the grass.

Heading straight for me.

Fuck. Not again.

"Here." The flowers land in front of me. "I'm sure Jorge could use them." Without waiting for my response, she spins on her heels and marches back. And I release the air held tight in my lungs.

I check the small tag peeking out, to confirm.

We are always thinking of you. The Reynolds family.

She can't even handle a simple gesture like flowers from us.

They stay for another half hour, both Livie and Darla talking to the tombs while Kacey stares off into nothing. I keep my head down the entire time, not wanting to attract her attention. Only when they pile into the car and drive away do I get up, settling the flowers from my parents back in between the two tombstones.

I've definitely learned something by coming here. That "forgiveness" isn't in Kacey's vocabulary.

Chapter 20

August 2012

Miami?

I give my eyes a good rub before checking my computer screen again. "How long was I asleep?" I mutter, checking the time stamps to the emails. They started at ten last night. Four emails in total between Kacey and a guy named Harry Tanner, property manager of an apartment building in Miami, Florida.

Where Kacey and Livie are apparently moving.

Next week.

"Fuck!" Miami is a helluva lot farther than Caledonia, Michigan. "Why?" There's not much to go on from the email. Kacey answered an ad on an online site, asking for a two-bedroom. When Tanner requested references, she said she'd pay him six months' rent upfront, cash. The subject line in his responding email said "Sold!"

And now they're moving to Miami.

What the hell happened? There's no way their aunt and uncle are okay with this. Livie's, what, fifteen? Just starting her sophomore year of high school?

Something must have happened.

I fall back into my chair with a heavy sigh, letting my eyes roll over the two-bedroom condo I bought almost a year ago, the walls still white and without a single picture hung. I just got a couch the other week. Before that, I was watching TV in an armchair. It's a place to stay, nothing more. It's never felt like *home*. And now it feels more like a trap.

How far away is Miami, exactly? I quickly type into Google. "Twenty-one hours to drive." My stomach sinks. I was actually considering getting a place out by Lansing and renting this out. So I could be closer to Kacey. Then I realized how fucking creepy that is.

Now she's moving to Miami. But for what?

Maybe to start over . . .

Maybe to let go of her past.

That could mean all kinds of things—good things. Like maybe she'll be ready to meet some guy. To let herself fall in love.

Unfolding the piece of lined paper that I've carried around in my pocket for over two years now, I read the words for the thousandth time and realize that I don't want her meeting some other guy. Falling in love with some other guy.

I want her to meet *me*. Trent Emerson. The guy who wants to feel the warmth that I know exists within her. The guy who's tied to her forever, whether she likes it or not. The one who needs to somehow make things right with her because I made everything so wrong.

Before I can fully think through what I'm doing, I've copied Tanner's email address into my own email and fired off a message, inquiring about an apartment.

By the time I'm out of the shower, I have a response. A one-bedroom is available beginning next week, if I have references.

I don't. But I have money. That's the thing about living the way I have for four years. Besides this condo and the Harley I bought three months ago after getting my motorcycle license, I haven't spent a dime. I've got plenty sitting in my account.

Enough to cover six months' rent.

In a matter of twenty minutes, I've secured a furnished one-bedroom apartment in the same building as Kacey Cleary, leaving me spinning. I was afraid this Tanner guy might get suspicious, having another person offer cash in place of references, and the exact same length of time. But if he is, he's not letting it get in the way of a deal.

Is this really happening? Yes, it is. And she's not going to ignore me anymore, I decide. I'm going to make her see me. But I can't rush this; I have to get it right. I'm only going to get one chance.

Chapter 21

I can barely hear anything with the blood rushing into my ears as I watch my new landlord lumber through the common area with Kacey and Livie trailing behind, pink suitcases bumping along the path. It's not much more than what I came with, given that I rode my bike down, figuring I'd just buy what I need.

For a few days there, I was afraid that I'd just handed Hank Tanner six months' rent for nothing. That Kacey would have bailed. There was nothing stopping her from backing out. Maybe she hadn't paid the guy upfront, after all.

But I can breathe now, because she's here.

Through the gauzy curtains, I see the awkward Tanner thumb toward my apartment and I instinctively take a step back. I'd kill to hear the conversation. Especially if it's anything like the "no orgies" rundown that he gave me before handing me my keys.

Within minutes, they've disappeared into the apartment beside mine.

And so I wait.

Tanner reappears a few minutes later, a fat envelope gripped within his meaty hand.

And . . . what now? Are they going to hang out in the courtyard? Do I just walk out and sit down beside them? No, that won't work.

After twenty minutes of pacing, I settle back into the desk that I'd strategically pulled up to the window so I could attempt to get some work done. As far as anyone knows, I'm in Rochester, working away in my home office. Luckily my mom doesn't do drop-ins. I stopped by her place the day before I left and gave her an extra-big hug, so big that I saw anxiety flickering in her eyes. I can't forget to text her every day.

I don't think she'll ever stop worrying about me. Not in the way a mother worries about her child. The way a mother worries about the son who should have died. Twice.

But I'm not going anywhere now, not when I'm sure I can help Kacey. I just need a chance.

And I get that chance. Hours later, after they've gone and come back with grocery bags dangling from their fingertips, the door slams shut and a flame of red passes by, a laundry basket with bedsheets in hand.

I dive for my own sheets, gathering them into a bundle, my jug of Tide in my free hand. And I head for the set of stairs that lead down to the laundry room. Machine doors slam on the other side and my heart begins racing. Am I really ready for this?

I can almost hear the note that sits in my back pocket answering me, giving me courage. The courage that I will need if I want to make her smile again. Because it's all I want to do.

To make her smile again.

Taking a deep breath, I push through the door.

Acknowledgments

This is an extremely sad story that for a long time I didn't see myself ever writing. But I'm glad that I decided to do it. It gives Trent a chance to explain himself—what he went through and why he did what he did, as crazy as some of it seems.

I have a few people to thank for their help getting me here.

To Treini Joris-Johnson, for your paramedics expertise. You helped me get that chaotic scene just right.

To my readers and my super-readers (the bloggers), for continuing along this journey with me, picking up my books, and for helping to spread the word.

To my street team, for your willingness to jump whenever I ask. You ladies are awesome.

To K. P. Simmon of Inkslinger PR, for dropping everything and calling me the moment I texted to tell you I was going to write Trent's story.

To my agent, Stacey Donaghy, for coming full-circle with me and this series (and going above and beyond).

To my editor, Sarah Cantin, for wanting this story. I actually knew where I was going with this before I started writing it! This is the first time (and probably the last time, so we should celebrate this).

To my publisher, Judith Curr, and the team at Atria Books: Ben Lee, Ariele Fredman, Tory Lowy, Kimberly Goldstein, and Alysha Bullock, for helping me get this story out.

To my husband and my girls, for tolerating a surprise book in my already busy schedule.

Turn the page for a peek at K.A. Tucker's novel
in her new series

BURYING WATER

JESSE

now

This can't be real . . . This can't be real . . . This can't be real . . .

The words cycle round and round in my mind like the wheels on my speeding 'Cuda as its ass-end slips and slides over the gravel and ice. This car is hard to handle on the best of days, built front-heavy and overloaded with horsepower. I'm going to put myself into one of these damn trees if I don't slow down.

I jam my foot against the gas pedal.

I *can't* slow down now.

Not until I know that Boone was wrong about what he claims to have overheard. His Russian is mediocre at best. I'll give anything for him to be wrong about *this*.

My gut clenches as my car skids around another turn, the cone shape of Black Butte looming like a monstrous shadow ahead of me in the pre-dawn light. The snowy tire tracks framed by my headlights might not even be the right ones, but they're wide like Viktor's Hummer and they're sure as hell the only ones down this old, deserted logging road. No one comes out here in January.

The line of trees marking the dead end comes up on me before I expect it. I slam on my brakes, sending my car sliding sideways toward the old totem pole. It's still sliding when I cut the rumbling engine, throw open the door, and jump out, fumbling with my flashlight. It takes three hard presses with my shaking hands to get the light to hold.

I begin searching the ground. The mess of tread marks tells me that someone pulled a U-turn. The footprints tell me that more than one person got out. And when I see the half-finished cigarette butt with that weird alphabet on the filter, I know Boone wasn't wrong.

"Alex!" My echo answers once . . . twice . . . before the vast wilderness swallows up my desperate cry. With frantic passes of my flashlight, my knuckles white against its body, I search the area until I spot the sets of footprints that lead off the old, narrow road and into the trees.

Frigid fingers curl around my heart.

Darting back to my car, I snatch the old red-and-blue plaid wool blanket that she loves so much from the backseat. Ice-cold snow packs into the sides of my sneakers as I chase the trail past the line of trees and into the barren field ahead, my blood rushing through my ears the only sound I process.

The only sign of life.

Raw fear numbs my senses, the Pacific Northwest winter numbs my body, but I push forward because if . . .

The beam of light passes over a still form lying facedown in the snow. I'd recognize that pink coat and platinum-blond hair of hers anywhere; the sparkly blue dress that she hates so much looks like a heap of sapphires against a white canvas.

My heart freezes.

"Alex." It's barely a whisper. I'm unable to produce more, my lungs giving up on me. I run, stumbling through the foot of snow until I'm on my knees and crawling forward to close the distance. A distance of no more than ten feet and yet one that seems like miles.

There's no mistaking the spray of crimson freckling the snow around her head. Or that most of her long hair is now dark and matted. Or that her silver stockings are torn and stained red, and a pool of blood has formed where her dress barely covers her thighs. Plenty of footprints mark the ground around her. He must have been here for a while.

I know that there are rules to follow, steps to make sure that I don't cause her further harm. But I ignore them because the sinking feeling in my stomach tells me I can't possibly hurt her more than he already has. I nestle her head with one hand while I slide the other under her shoulder. I roll her over.

Cold shock knocks the wind out of me.

I've never seen anybody look like *this*.

I scoop her limp body into my arms, cradling the once beautiful face that I've seen in every light—rage to ecstasy and the full gamut in between—yet is now unrecognizable. Placing two blood-coated fingers over her throat, I wait. Nothing.

A light pinch against her lifeless wrist. Nothing.

Maybe a pulse does exist but it's hidden, masked by my own racing one.

Then again, by the look of her, likely not.

One . . . two . . . three . . . plump, serene snowflakes begin floating down from the unseen sky above. Soon, they will converge and cover the tracks, the blood. The evidence. Mother Nature's own blanket to hide the unsightly blemish in her yard.

"I'm so sorry." I don't try to restrain the hot tears as they roll down my cheeks to land on her mangled lips—lips I had stolen plenty of kisses from, back when I was too stupid to realize how dangerous that really was. This is my fault. She had warned me. If I had just listened, had stayed away from her, had not told her how I felt . . .

. . . had not fallen wildly in love with her.

I lean down to steal a kiss even now, the coppery taste of her blood mixing with my salty tears. "I'm so damn sorry. I should never have even looked your way," I manage to get out around my sobs, tucking the blanket she loved to curl up in over her.

An almost inaudible gasp slips out. A slight breeze against my mouth more than anything else.

My lungs freeze, my eyes glued to her, afraid to hope. "Alex?" Is it possible?

A moment later, a second gasp—a wet, rattling sound—escapes.

She's not dead.

Not yet, anyway.

ONE

ALEX

in between

A fire.

The fragrance calls to me.

I cannot see, for my eyes are sealed shut against the wicked glow in his stare.

I cannot hear, for my ears have blocked out his appalling promises.

I cannot feel, for my body has long since shattered.

But, as I lie in the cool stillness of the night, waiting for my final peace, that comforting waft of burning bark and twigs and crispy leaves encases me.

It whispers to me that everything will be okay.

And I so desperately long to believe it.

———

Beep . . .

". . . basilar skull fracture . . ."

Beep . . .

". . . collapsed lung . . ."

Beep . . .

". . . ruptured spleen . . ."

Beep . . .

". . . frostbite . . ."

Beep . . .

Beep . . .

"Will she live?"

Beep . . .

"I honestly don't know how she has survived this long."

Beep . . .

"We need to keep this quiet for now."

"Gabe, you just showed up on the doorstep of my hospital with a half-dead girl. How am I supposed to do that?"

"You just do. Call me if she wakes up. No one questions her but me. *No one,* Meredith."

————

"Don't try to talk yet," someone—a woman—warns softly. I can't see her. I can't see anything; my lids open to mere slits, enough to admit a haze of light and a flurry of activity around me—gentle fingertips, low murmurs, papers rustling.

And then that rhythmic beep serenades me back into oblivion.

TWO

JANE DOE

now

I don't know how I got here.

I don't know where here is.

I hurt.

Who is this woman hovering over me?

"Please page Dr. Alwood immediately," she calls to someone unseen. Turning back to look at me, it takes her a long moment before she manages a white-toothed smile. Even in my groggy state, there's no missing the pity in it. Her chest lifts with a deep breath and then she shifts her attention to the clear-fluid bags hanging on a rack next to me. "Glad to finally see your eyes open," she murmurs. "They're a really pretty russet color." The hem of her lilac uniform grazes the cast around my hand.

My cast.

I take inventory of the room—the pale beige walls, the stiff chairs, the pastel-blue curtain. The machines. It finally clicks.

I'm in a hospital.

"How—" I stall over the question as that first word scratches against my throat.

"You were intubated to help you breathe. That hoarseness will go away soon, I promise."

I needed help *breathing*?

"You're on heavy doses of morphine, so you may feel a little disoriented right now. That's normal. Here." A cool hand slips under my neck as she fluffs up my pillow.

"Where am I?" I croak out, just now noticing that bandages are dividing my face in two at the nose.

"You're at St. Charles in Bend, Oregon, with the very best doctors that we have. It looks like you're going to pull through." Again, another smile. Another sympathetic stare. She's a pretty, young woman, her long, light brown hair pulled back in a ponytail, her eyes a mesmerizing leafy green.

Not mesmerizing enough to divert me from her words. Pull through *what* exactly?

She prattles on about the hospital, the town, the unusually brisk winter weather. I struggle to follow along, too busy grappling with my memory, trying to answer the litany of questions swirling inside my mind. Nothing comes, though. I'm drawing a complete blank.

Like she said, it must be the morphine.

A creak pulls my gaze to the far corner of the room, where a tall, lanky woman in a white coat covering a pink floral shirt has just entered. With quick, long strides she rounds my bed, drawing the curtain behind her as she approaches. "Hello."

I'm guessing this is the doctor whom the nurse had paged. I watch as she fishes out a clip from her pocket and pins back a loose strand of apricot-colored hair. Snapping on a pair of surgical gloves, she then pulls a small flashlight from her pocket. "How are you feeling?"

"I'm not sure yet." My voice is rough but at least audible. "Are you my doctor? Doctor . . ." I read the name on the badge affixed to her coat. "Alwood?"

Green eyes rimmed with dark circles search mine for a long moment. "Yes, I operated on you. My name is Dr. Meredith Alwood." I squint against the beam of light from her flashlight, first into my left eye and then my right. "Are you in any pain?"

"I don't know. I'm . . . sore. And confused." My tongue catches something rough against my bottom lip and I instinctively run my tongue along it, sensing a piece of thread. It's when I begin toying with it that I also notice the wide gap on the right side of my mouth. I'm missing several teeth.

"Good. I'm glad. Not about the confused part." Dr. Alwood's lips press together in a tight smile. "But you'd be a lot more than 'sore' if the pain meds weren't working."

My throat burns. I swallow several times, trying to alleviate the dryness. "What happened? How did I get here?" Someone must know something. Right?

Dr. Alwood opens her mouth but then hesitates. "Amber, you have your rounds to finish, don't you?"

The nurse, who's been busy replacing the various bags on the IV stand, stops to look at the doctor for a long second, her delicately drawn eyebrows pulled together. They have the same green eye color, I notice. In fact, they have the exact same al-mond-shaped eyes and straight-edged nose.

Or, maybe I'm just hallucinating, thanks to the drugs.

Kind fingers probe something unseen on my scalp and then, with the sound of the door clicking shut, the doctor asks, "How about we start with the basic questions. Can you please give me your name?"

I open my mouth to answer. It's such a simple question. Everyone has a name. *I* have a name. And yet . . . "I don't . . . I don't know," I stammer. How do I not know what my name is? I'm sure it's the same name I've had all my life.

My life.

What do I remember about my life? Shouldn't *something* about it be registering?

A wave of panic surges through me and the EKG's telltale beep increases its cadence. Why can't I seem to recall a single scrap of my life?

Not a face, not a name, not a childhood pet.

Nothing.

Dr. Alwood stops what she's doing to meet my gaze. "You've had a significant head injury. Just try to relax." Her words come slow and steady. "I'll tell you what I know. Maybe that will jog your memory. Okay? Just take a few breaths first." She's quick to add, "Not too deep."

I do as instructed, watching my chest lift and fall beneath my blue-and-white checkered gown, cringing with a sharp twinge of pain on my right side with each inhale. Finally, that incessant beeping begins to slow.

I turn my attention back to her. Waiting.

"You were found in the parking lot of an abandoned building nine days ago," Dr. Alwood begins.

I've been here for nine days?

"You were brought into the emergency room by ambulance with extensive, life-threatening trauma to your body. Your injuries were consistent with a physical assault. You had several fractures—to your ribs, your left leg, your right arm, your skull. Your right lung collapsed. You required surgery for a hematoma, a ruptured spleen, and lacerations to . . ." Her calm voice drifts off into obscurity as she recites a laundry list of brutality that can't possibly have my name at the top of it. "It will take some time to recover from all of these injuries. Do you feel any tightness in your chest now, when you inhale?"

I swallow the rising lump in my throat, not sure how to answer. I'm certainly having difficulty breathing, but I think it has more to do with panic than anything else.

"No," I finally offer. "I think I'm okay."

"Good." She gingerly peels back pieces of gauze from my face—some over the bridge of my nose and another piece running along the right side of my face, from my temple all the way down to my chin. By the slight nod of approval, I'm guessing she's happy with whatever is beneath. "And how is the air flow through your nose? Any stuffiness?"

I test my nostrils out. "A little."

She stops her inspection to scribble something on the chart that's sitting on the side table. "You were very fortunate that Dr. Gonzalez was in Bend on a ski trip. He's one of the leading plastic surgeons in the country and a very good friend of mine. When I saw you come in, I called him right away. He offered us his skill, pro bono."

A part of me knows that I should be concerned that I needed a plastic surgeon for my face, and yet I'm more concerned with the fact that I can't even imagine what that face looks like.

"I removed the stitches two days ago to help minimize the scarring. You may need a secondary surgery on your nose, depending on how it heals. We won't know until the swelling goes down." Setting the clipboard down on the side table again, she asks, "Do you remember *anything* about what happened to you?"

"No." *Nothing.*

The combination of her clenched jaw and the deep furrow across her forehead gives me the feeling that she's about to deliver more bad news. "I'm sorry to tell you that we found evidence of sexual assault."

I feel the blood drain from my face and the steady beeping spikes again as my heart begins to pound in my chest. "I don't . . . I don't understand." She's saying I was . . . raped? Somebody touched me like *that*? The urge to curl my arms around my body and squeeze my legs tight swarms me, but I'm too sore to act on it. How could I possibly not remember being *raped*?

"I need to examine the rest of your injuries." Dr. Alwood waits for my reluctant nod and then slides the flannel sheet down and lifts my hospital gown. I'm temporarily distracted by the cast around my leg as she gently peels back the bandages around my ribs and the left side of my stomach.

"These look good. Now, just relax, I'll make this quick," she promises, nudging my free leg toward the edge of my bed. I distract myself from my discomfort with the tiled ceiling above as she gently inspects me. "You required some internal stitching, but everything should heal properly with time. We're still running some tests and blood work, but we've ruled out the majority of sexually transmitted diseases. We also completed a rape kit on you."

I close my eyes as a tear slips out from the corner of one eye, the salt from it burning my sensitive skin. Why did this happen to me? Who could have done such a thing?

Raped . . . STDs . . . "What about . . . I mean, could I be pregnant?" The question slips out unbidden.

True to her promise, Dr. Alwood quickly readjusts my gown and covers. Peeling off her gloves, she tosses them in the trash bin and then takes a seat on the edge of my bed. "We can certainly rule that out from the rape." She pauses. "Because you were already pregnant when you were brought in."

The air sails from my lungs as she delivers yet *another* harsh punch of news. My gaze drifts to my flat abdomen. I have a baby in there?

"You were about ten weeks along."

Were. Past tense.

"Do you not recall *any* of this?" Dr. Alwood's brows draw together as she watches me closely.

A soft "no" slips out and I can't help but feel that she doesn't believe me.

"Well, given your extensive injuries, it is not at all surprising that you miscarried. You're lucky to be alive, as it is." She hesitates before she adds, "I don't think that whoever did this to you intended for you to survive."

A strange cold sweeps through my limbs as I take in the ruined body lying on this bed before me. I've been lucid for all of five minutes—the long hand on the clock ahead tells me that—and in that short time, this doctor has informed me that I was beaten, raped, . . . and left for dead.

And I lost a baby I don't even remember carrying, or making.

I don't know who the father was.

I don't even know who *I* am.

"I'm going to send you for another CT scan and MRI." I feel the weight of her gaze on me. "Are you sure there isn't someone or something that you remember? A husband? Or a boyfriend? Or a sibling? A parent? Maybe a city where you grew up? The hospital would like to find your family for you."

Her barrage of questions only makes my heart rate spike and the annoying EKG ramp up again. I can't answer a single one of them. Is anyone missing me right now? Are they searching for me? Am I from Bend, Oregon, or do I live somewhere else?

Dr. Alwood sits quietly, waiting, as I focus on a small yellow splotch on the ceiling. That's water damage. How can I recognize *that* and not my own name?

"Even a tiny detail?" she presses, the urgency in her voice soft and pleading.

"No." There's nothing.

I remember nothing at all.

THREE

JESSE

then

There are a lot of things I don't like about Portland.

The rain tops the list.

Scratch that. *Driving* in the rain tops the list. It's usually just a dreary never-ending drizzle, but once in a while the skies open up for an especially heavy downpour. The shitty old Toyota I bought for five hundred bucks doesn't deal well with that weather, the engine randomly sputtering and cutting out like it's drowning. I don't know how many times I've tried to fix the problem.

September was a heavy month for rain. It looks like October is competing for a record, too, because it's pouring again tonight. It's only a matter of time before the car gives out on me, right here in the middle of this deserted road. Then I'll be just like the poor sucker on the shoulder up ahead, his hazards flashing.

Even though I've already made my mind up to keep moving, when I realize it's a BMW Z8, my foot eases off the gas pedal. I've never seen one in real life before. Probably because there are only a few thousand in the entire country and each one would go for a pretty penny. It's rare and it's fucking gorgeous.

And it has a flat tire.

"Nope." Changing tires in the rain sucks. That rich bastard can wait for roadside assistance to come save him. I'm sold on that plan until my headlights catch long blond hair in the driver's side. Twenty feet past, my conscience takes over and I can't help but brake. "Shit," I mutter, pulling off to the shoulder and slowly backing up.

No one's getting out, but if she's alone, she's probably wary. With a loud groan, I step out into the rain, yanking the hood of my gray sweatshirt up over my head. I jog over to the passenger-side window. Growing up with a sheriff as a father, you learn never to stand on the road, even if there isn't a car in sight. People get clipped all the time.

I knock against the glass.

And wait.

"Come on . . ." I mutter, my head hung low, the rain pounding on my back feeling like a cold hose bath. It can't be more than 40 degrees out here. Another five seconds and I'm leaving her here.

Finally the window cracks open, just enough for me to peer through. She's alone in the car. It's dark, but I'm pretty sure I see tears. I definitely see smeared black makeup. And her eyes . . . They glisten with fear. I don't blame her. She's driving a high-priced car and she's sitting alone out here after eleven at night. And now there's a guy in a hoodie hanging outside her window. I adjust my tone accordingly. "Do you need help?"

I hear her swallow hard before answering, "Yes. I do." She sounds young, but it's hard to tell with some women.

"Have you called Triple-A?"

She hesitates and then shakes her head.

Okay . . . not very talkative. She smells incredible, though, based on the flowery perfume wafting out of her car. Incredible and rich. "Your spare's in the trunk?"

"I . . . think so?"

I sigh. Looks like I'm changing a tire in the pouring rain after all. "Okay. Pop your trunk and I'll see what I can do. Stay in here."

I round the car. Beneath half a dozen shopping bags and under the trunk floor, I find the spare tucked away. Running back to get my jack and flashlight out of my car—I use my own tools whenever I can—I settle down by the back corner of the Z8, happy for the dead roads. Not one vehicle has passed since I stopped.

The BMW is jacked and the lug nuts are off when the driver's door opens. "I'll have this changed in another two minutes!" I holler, gently pulling the rim off. "You should stay inside."

The door slams shut—I cringe, you don't slam anything on a car like this!—and then heels click on the pavement as she comes around to stand next to me. The rain suddenly stops pelting my back. "Is that better?" she asks in a soft voice.

I don't need to glance up to know that there's an umbrella hovering over me. "You're not from Portland, are you?" I mumble with a smile. Neither am I, technically, but I've learned to adapt in the four years that I've lived here. Part of that is knowing that no guy in Portland would be caught dead using an umbrella. Neither would most women, actually. We'd rather duck our head and get wet than be labeled a wuss. Smart? No.

"No, not originally."

I yank the tire off and roll it to the side. That's when my eyes get caught up in a pair of long, bare legs right beside me, covered in goose bumps from the cold. Forcing my head back down with a low exhale, I grab the spare.

"Thank you for stopping. Most people wouldn't have."

Most people, including me. "You should really get a Triple-A plan."

"I have one," she admits somberly and then, after a second's hesitation, adds, "My phone died and I can't find my car charger."

So, she was *totally* stranded. As much as this sucks, I'm glad I stopped. This should give my conscience something to feel good about, seeing as I've tested it plenty over the years. "I can't find my phone charger half the time. It's usually under the seat. I finally went and bought a second cord that I keep in my glove compartment."

I hear the smile in her voice as she says, "I'll have to remember that."

"Yeah, you should. Especially in a car like this." The spare is bolted in place in another minute.

"You're very fast."

I smirk as I lower the car. "I've been changing tires since I could walk." Well, not really, but it feels like it. Grabbing the flat tire with one arm, I intentionally step out from the umbrella so I don't get her dirty with it on my way to the trunk. It's too late for me, but I'm used to it. I go through more clothes than the average guy. "Do you have far to go? These aren't meant for long distances."

"About ten miles."

"Good. I can stay behind you until you get off the highway, if that makes you feel better," I offer, wiping my wet, dirty hands against my jeans. "I'm headed that way anyway."

"That's very kind of you." She doesn't make a move to leave, though. She just stands there, her face hidden by the darkness and that giant umbrella.

And then I hear the stifled sob.

Ah, shit. I don't know what to do with a rich girl crying on the side of the road. Or crying girls in general. I've made plenty of them do it, unintentionally, and felt bad about it after. But other than saying, "I'm sorry," I'm at a loss. I hesitate before asking, "Is everything okay? I mean, do you have someone you can call? You can use my phone if you want. I'll grab it from the car."

"No, I don't have anyone."

A long, lingering silence hangs over us.

"Well . . ." I really just want to get home and catch *The Late Show*, but I didn't get soaked so I could leave her standing out here.

"Are you happy?" Her question cuts through the quiet night like a rude interruption.

"Uh . . ." *What?* I shift nervously on my feet.

"In your life. Are you happy? Or do you ever wish you could just start over?"

I frown into the darkness. "Right now I wish I wasn't freezing my ass off in the rain," I admit. What the hell else do I say to that? I wasn't ready for deep, thought-provoking questions. I generally avoid those, and God knows the idiots I hang out with don't toss them around. Is this chick out of her mind?

She steps in closer, lifting her umbrella to shield, granting me part of my wish. "I mean, if you could just start over fresh . . . *free* yourself from all the bad decisions you've made . . . would you do it?"

Obviously this woman's shitty day started long before the flat tire. "Sounds like you have some regrets," I finally offer. It's not really an answer to her question but, honestly, I don't know how to respond to that.

"Yeah. I think I do." It's so soft, I barely hear her over the rain hitting asphalt and the low rumble of her idling engine. I startle as cool fingers suddenly slide over my cheek, my nose, my jaw—covered in fresh stubble—until they find my mouth, where they rest in a strangely intimate way. I feel like she's testing me. What's going on in this woman's head right now?

Though I can't stop the steady climb of my heartbeat, I don't move a single muscle, more curious than anything. Very slowly, the shadow in front of me shifts closer and closer, until her mouth is hovering over mine and her breathing is shaky.

And then she kisses me.

It's a tentative kiss at first, her lips lightly sweeping across mine without committing entirely, but it gets my blood rushing all the same. I can't say that I've ever kissed a woman without seeing her face first. It's both unnerving and strangely liberating.

If she looks anything like her lips feel, then I'm kissing a super-model right now.

Finally she finds her place, her lips slightly parted as they gently work against mine, each one of her ragged breaths like an intoxicating spell as they slip into my mouth alongside her tongue. I don't even care about the rain or the cold or getting home anymore, too busy fighting the urge to loose my hands on her. But I don't know why the fuck she's doing this and I'm a suspicious person by nature. So, I ball my fists and keep my arms to my sides while her mouth slowly teases mine and her hand grasps the side of my face.

Just when I'm ready to give up on my mistrust and pull her into me, she suddenly breaks free, her short, hard pants dispelling her calm. She steps back, taking the shield of her umbrella with her. The cold rain is a semi-effective douse to the heat coursing through my body.

"Thank you."

I smile into the darkness. "No big deal. Tires take me no time."

"I wasn't talking about the tire." She's smiling too. I can hear it in her soft words.

With my mouth hanging open, I watch her silhouette round the car. In one fluid motion, she folds her umbrella up and slides into the driver's seat.

And I'm left standing here, wondering what the hell just happened. She doesn't know what I look like either. We could pass each other on the sidewalk and we'd never know.

Maybe that's the point.

Shaking my head, I dart back to my car, my clothes soaked and my mind thoroughly mystified. She may be sweet but if she goes around kissing strange men on the side of the road, no wonder she has regrets. I hope regrets are the worst thing she ever has to deal with.

True to my word, I tail her for eight miles, my fingers testing my lips as I recall the feel of hers against them, until she signals toward one of Portland's richer areas. A big part of me wants to turn off and follow her the rest of the way. Just so I know who she is.

I have my hand on the turn signal. But at the last minute, I pull back and keep heading straight. Regrets have a tendency to spread when you tie yourself to the wrong kind of person. I've learned that the hard way.

I hope she finds what she's looking for.

FOUR

JANE DOE

now

"I told you already; she's not lying. She doesn't remember *a thing*! Anyone who looks into the poor girl's eyes can see that!"

Dr. Alwood's harsh tone pulls me out of a light sleep. She's standing next to my bed, squared off against a man with an olive complexion and wavy chestnut-brown hair—peppered with gray at the temples—and a grim expression, dusted with day-old scruff.

"I have to do my job, Meredith," the man says, his dark eyes shifting to catch me watching. With a nod in my direction, he clears his throat.

Dr. Alwood turns and her scowl vanishes, replaced by a soft smile. Today she's wearing a baby-blue blouse tucked under her white coat. It doesn't do much for her pallid complexion, but it's pretty all the same. "I'm sorry to wake you," she says, her voice returning to its typical calm. A life jacket for me these past few days, while submerged in this ongoing nightmare. "The sheriff would like to speak with you." With a gesture to the man, she introduces him. "This is Sheriff Welles, of Deschutes County."

The man offers me a curt smile before dipping his head forward and squeezing his eyes shut. As if he has to regroup; as if facing me for more than that short period of time is difficult. Maybe it is. Based on what the small parade of nurses coming in and out of my room have told me, the swelling has gone down and the deep purple bruising has faded. You can even see my high cheekbones again, whatever that means. I have yet to even glimpse myself in a mirror and no one seems to be in a rush to bring one to my bedside, not even to see if it may trigger my memory. They keep telling me that we should wait "just a few more days."

"He's going to ask you a *few* questions." She casts a glare his way. "Right, Gabe?"

His heavyset brow pulls together as he lifts his gaze to meet mine again. Such penetrating eyes—not a single fleck of gold or brown to break up the near-black color. They draw me in and make me hold my breath at the same time. He must do well in interrogations. "Right."

Gabe Welles. Of course, the sheriff knows what his name is. Everyone knows what their name is. I'm the only clueless one around here. "I don't know how much help I can be," I say, my voice much smoother than when I first regained conscious-ness . . . my eyes flicker to the clock to calculate . . . forty-two hours ago. I've regained nothing else.

I still have no idea who I am and I certainly don't remember being raped and beaten. I imagine most victims like me would do anything, take any sort of pill or potion, to forget the traumatic experience. But I've spent every conscious moment grappling with the recesses of my mind, hoping to find a thread to grab on to, to tug, something that will unravel the mystery.

Nothing. I remember nothing.

"You seem to be doing much better than the last time I saw you," Sheriff Welles says in a rich, gravelly voice that demands attention.

"Gabe—I mean, Sheriff Welles—was the one who found you," Dr. Alwood explains.

My cheeks heat with color. "How bad was I? I mean . . . ?" *Was I on bloody, naked display for him to see?* Do I even want to know if I was? It should be the least of my worries, and yet the thought churns my stomach.

"I've seen a lot in my thirty-five years in the police force, but . . . you were in rough shape." He pauses to clear his throat. "Dr. Alwood has already informed me that you don't recall anything. I have something that I thought may help." From a canvas bag, he pulls out a clear plastic package marked "Evidence," followed by a case number, and holds it up. Electric-blue sequined material stares back at me. "You were wearing this dress when I found you."

Where would I be going in that? A wedding? A disco? Based on the reddish-brown stains and tears, I won't be wearing it ever again. The sheriff and doctor watch me closely as I admit, "I don't recognize it."

He dumps it back into the canvas bag and pulls out another plastic evidence bag, this one with a light pink coat and very clearly covered in blood. "You were wearing this over your dress."

Was I? "It's not familiar," I answer honestly. The steady pulse from the EKG begins to increase again. I've noticed that it does that every time Dr. Alwood begins questioning me, as my agitation rises.

He pulls out a third bag, with only one silver dress shoe in it. It has a heel so high, no sane human would choose to wear it. "Just like Cinderella," I murmur half-heartedly, adding, "I don't even know how I could walk in that."

Without a word, he holds up a small bag with a necklace in it. Even in the muted fluorescent lighting above, the stones sparkle like stars. "We had these diamonds inspected. Whoever bought this isn't hurting for cash," Sheriff Welles says.

"I don't know who that would be," I answer honestly. Is that person me? Am *I* wealthy? Or is the person who gave that to me rich? Who would have given that to me? The father of my lost child, perhaps? Where is he *now*? I instinctively glance at my hands. At the fingertips that reach out from one end of my cast, the remnants of my red nail polish still visible though my nails are badly broken. Half of my pinky nail has torn off. If I look very carefully, I *think* I can make out a tan line on the third finger of my right hand. "Was I wearing a ring?"

"Why do you ask? Do you remember wearing a ring?" His voice has dropped an octave, almost lulling. As if he's hoping to coax an answer out of me.

I frown. "No. I just . . . If I was pregnant, does that mean I'm married?" Did I walk down an aisle in a white dress and profess my love to someone? Am I even old enough to be married?

"This was the only piece of jewelry that we found on you," Sheriff Welles confirms.

"Could my ring have been stolen?"

"I can't say for sure, but my experience tells me that, had this been a robbery-motivated attack, they would not have left this necklace behind."

Not robbery.

If not that, then *why*?

Why?

Why would someone do this to me?

Dr. Alwood and Sheriff Welles sit and wait while a thousand questions flood my mind and tears of fear and frustration burn my eyes. I gather they're waiting for me to be struck by an epiphany thanks to a couple of plastic bags stuffed with bloody clothes and jewels. They don't seem to understand, though. My memory—my life—isn't simply riddled with holes. It has been sucked into a black hole, leaving nothing but this battered husk behind, my mind spinning but unable to gain traction.

Finally, I can't take it anymore. I burst out with, "I'm not lying! I don't remember who I am!"

A wisp of a sigh escapes the sheriff as he drops the jewelry back into the bag, his gaze touching Dr. Alwood's eyes in the process, an unreadable communication between them. "Okay, Jay—" He cuts himself off.

"It's okay; you can call me that," I mutter through a sniffle. I've overheard the nurses referring to me as "JD" a few times and, when I finally asked Dr. Alwood about it, she admitted with a grimace that it stands for "Jane Doe." Because that's who I am now.

Jane Doe.

Apparently that's not just reserved for people with toe tags.

He pauses, settling his stern gaze on me. "I wish I had more to tell you about what happened, but I don't. We believe that you were dumped in the location where we found you. Where you were attacked, I can't say. We've canvassed the area for clues, but nothing's come up. We don't even have good tire tracks to work with; the fresh snowfall covered them. No witnesses have come forward yet and no one has filed a missing person's report that matches your case. I have my men scouring the database."

He sighs. "The rape test returned no results. There were no DNA matches in there. Dr. Alwood was able to order a DNA test on your unborn fetus. Again, results did not match anything in the database."

I guess that means that the father wasn't a criminal. At least there's that. "So . . . that's it?"

His jaw tightens and then he offers me only a curt nod.

My eyes drift away from both of them to the window across from me, the sky beyond painted a deceptively cheerful blue. The small television mounted on the wall is still on—I fell asleep watching it—and showing a news broadcast. Yellow caution tape circles a gas station. A caption flashes along the bottom, calling for witnesses.

And a thought hits me. "Was my story on the news?"

"No." Sheriff Welles's head shakes firmly. "I've kept this story away from the media." He adds in a low mutter, "God knows they'd love to have it."

"But maybe it would reach my . . . family?" The family who hasn't filed a report yet?

"Yes, maybe. Maybe it'll also reach the person who attacked you. Do you want him to know that you survived?"

A cold wave rushes through me as Dr. Alwood snaps, "Gabe!"

His mouth purses together but he presses on. "Reporters will sensationalize this story. They'll want pictures of your face. They'll want to post details of your attack. Do *you* want that all over the news?"

"No." My eyes dart to the door as a spark of panic hits me. "You don't think he'd come here for me, do you?" Maybe he already has. Maybe my attacker has already stood there, watching me as I've slept. I shiver against the icy chill that courses through my body with the thought.

"I think he assumes you died and your remains would be dragged off by a mountain lion or wolves before they were discovered," he assures me, his words offering little comfort. "That old tannery building probably hasn't had a visitor in over a year."

"How'd you find me, then?"

"Sheer luck," he answers without missing a beat. "I have a police officer stationed outside your door just as a precaution. We'll keep you safe. If you do remember something, no matter how small, please let either Dr. Alwood or me know immediately." The way he names himself and the doctor—slowly and precisely—I get the distinct impression that he meant to swap "either" for "only."

With my reluctant nod, he heads toward the door.

"I'll be back in a moment," Dr. Alwood says. I watch her trail Sheriff Welles out to stand behind my door. Thanks to the window, I can see them exchanging words, their lips moving fast, their foreheads pulled tight. Neither seems happy. And then Sheriff Welles leans forward to place a quick peck on Dr. Alwood's cheek before disappearing from my view.

Suddenly the slips of "Gabe" and the terse tone you wouldn't expect a doctor to use with the sheriff make sense.

"Are you two married?" I ask the second Dr. Alwood pushes back through the door, glancing down to see that her fingers are free of any jewelry.

"For twenty-nine years. Some days being married to the town sheriff is easy, and . . ." she collects my chart from the side table and hangs it back on the end of my bed, a corner of her mouth kicking up in a tiny smirk, "other days, not so much."

I think about that extravagant necklace I was wearing, and the ring that I was not. "I guess I wasn't married to the father of my baby." Had I been happy when I found out I was pregnant? Was the father happy? Did he even know?

Is he the one who did this to me?

Dr. Alwood heaves a sigh as she begins pushing buttons on the heart rate monitor. The lights dim. "Your heart is strong. We don't need this anymore." With cool hands, she peels the various electrodes from my chest, my arms, and my thighs, as she explains, "It isn't uncommon to see patients with amnesia after a brain injury. It's more commonly anterograde versus retrograde, but . . ." She must see the confusion on my face because she quickly clarifies, "You're more likely to struggle with your short-term memory than long-term memory. And, when it is retrograde, the gaps are usually spotty, or isolated to specific events. It's *extremely* rare to see a complete lapse in memory like yours, especially one that lasts this long. Your tests have come back showing normal brain activity and no permanent damage."

I feel the pull against the raw scar on the side of my face as I frown. If it's not brain injury, then . . . "What does that mean?"

"I think it may be psychological."

"What does *that* mean?" Is the doctor saying I'm crazy?

"It means that whatever happened was traumatic enough to make you *want* to forget everything about your life." Her eyes drift over my body. "Given what I've seen, I can believe it. But on a positive note, you're more than likely to overcome this. Brain injuries tend to have long-lasting effects."

"So you're saying I'll remember something soon?" I hold my breath, waiting for her to promise me that I'll be fine again.

"Maybe." She hesitates. "Unfortunately, this is not within my expertise. I've referred you to an excellent psychologist, though. Hopefully she can give us some answers."

"What if she can't? What if I never remember anything?" What if I simply . . . *exist* in the present?

"Let's meet with Dr. Weimer before you worry too much," she says, reaching forward to rest a hand on my leg cast. Given that her interaction with me up until now has always been friendly but on the extreme professional level, this feels both foreign and welcome. Dr. Alwood may be the only person in the world right now that I trust.

That's probably why the question slips out in a whisper. "Did I do something to deserve this?" It's a rhetorical question. She can't answer that, any more than she can tell me who attacked me, who raped me, who left me for dead next to an abandoned building. But I ask it anyway.

She shakes her head. "I can't believe that there is anything you could have done to deserve *this*, Jane."

Jane. I don't like the name. Not at all. That's not Dr. Alwood's fault, though. What else are they going to call me?

"Thank you." I sound so small, so weak. So . . . insignificant. Am I? "*Someone* must be missing me. Even just *one person*, right?" I can't be all alone in this world, can I?

Dr. Alwood's face crumbles into a sad smile. "Yes, Jane. I'm quite certain that there is someone who misses you dearly."

Get email updates on

K.A. TUCKER,

exclusive offers,

and other great book recommendations

from Simon & Schuster.

Visit **newsletters.simonandschuster.com**

or

scan below to sign up: